C

Embrace

Emily Walters

Christmas Embrace

Published by Emily Walters

Copyright © 2019 by Emily Walters

ISBN 978-1-07503-307-0

First printing, 2019

www.EmilyWaltersBooks.com

PRINTED IN THE UNITED STATES OF AMERICA

Dedication

I want to dedicate this book to my beloved husband, who makes every day in my life worthwhile. Thank you for believing in me when nobody else does, giving me encouragement when I need it the most, and loving me simply for being myself.

Table of Contents

Chapter 1

Sarah Armstrong sat at her desk, pencil in hand, staring at the notebook in front of her. She had a laptop open to her left, and a cup of coffee with cream and sugar to her right. Sarah was in her writing mode, thinking up new ideas for her next article. She hadn't been able to think of a topic that she felt was worthy of the magazine in a week. Plus it was a week till Christmas, and her holiday deadlines were coming up.

She took a sip of her coffee, and an idea about a possible article struck her. Her head shot up and her eyes widened as she started to scribble on the blank paper, before stopping halfway. She grumbled as she crossed out her idea and sighed exasperatedly. "Why can't I think of anything!?" She furiously brushed a piece of stray blonde hair out of her face.

Sarah was usually an excellent writer, and the articles she penned often made it into the magazine's main features. She enjoyed her job very much, and wouldn't give it up for the world. Though sometimes she would hit these roadblocks, she usually got past them.

There was a knock on the wall of her cubicle, and Sarah looked up. It was her manager, Terrence Evans, the founder of Rumor, the tabloid magazine where Sarah worked as a journalist. "Come in," Sarah said as she put her pencil down and locked her bright blue eyes onto his green ones. It looked like Terrence had something on his mind, and hadn't come just for a social visit.

She and Terrence had a very professional relationship. He was a no-nonsense kind of guy, and she respected it. He had built Rumor from nothing, and had made it rather successful. He expected a lot from his employees, and Sarah definitely tried her best to meet all of his expectations. Sarah always met all her deadlines and wrote successful articles. She prided herself on them, and always wanted to improve.

Sarah remembered her interview, a year and a half ago, when she had first come to the building that Rumor worked out of. She had just come to New York City and as a twenty-three- year-old in a big city, she was feeling rather overwhelmed. She had moved because she wanted to advance her career and write for a bigger magazine. She had worked at a magazine in her old town, but there was no future there for her, no place to grow.

Terrence had been friendly, yet firm during their first meeting. She had been ecstatic when he called her back, asking her to start working. She dreamed of being the best in the journalism field, which was a very difficult task. Pulse was an important step in that journey.

"Still working on creating a new article?" Terrence said as he sat down in the chair opposite to Sarah's.

"Yeah, I am… Unfortunately not making much headway." She sighed.

"Well, then I bring good news." Terrence grinned as he pulled out his phone and pressed a couple times onto the screen. "I may have your next article, right here."

"Oh?" Sarah smiled. "Care to share?"

"Well… you know Hamilton and Ryan Clouse, right?"

"Of course!" Sarah knew them very well, as did most of the tabloid reporters. They were the famous sons of Roger Clouse, the billionaire businessman. Ryan Clouse, the younger brother, was the one featured most often in the magazines. He was a troublemaker, and his relationship status was often broadcasted in the headlines as he frequently changed girlfriends, sometimes as often as once a week.

Hamilton, the more mature brother, wasn't as popular as Ryan in the tabloids, or as young, but he was attractive in his own way. He, at twenty-nine, was one of the most successful business executives at his father's firm, Clouse Industries. He was still single, having devoted all his time to rising quickly in the firm. He worked hard, even though he probably didn't have to because of his last name. Without it, it would have been near impossible for him to be so successful at such a young age. He was brilliant, but readers of the magazine were more interested in the escapades of Ryan.

"So, what about the Clouses?" she asked.

"I just received a tip-off, from one of our accurate sources. She says that four days from now, *all* of the Clouses will be heading to their winter mansion. And that Ryan will be bringing his new girlfriend with him there. No one's ever seen them together before, and if you can get a couple of shots of them, then it'll be a big scoop," Terrence explained the good news.

Sarah thought about it. "Yes, I'll do it," she said after a second.

Terrence's phone pinged, signifying that a new text had come. "Oh! And now she's telling me that Ryan may *propose* at the mansion! You have to get some pictures. This will be big if we're the first ones. This is vital, Sarah, I'll need this article and the photos done as soon as possible. This is *very important*." He emphasized very heavily on the last two words. "I'll email you the rest of the information, as to location and what pictures and info I want you to gather." He stood up, ready to leave.

"Thank you, Terrence. I won't mess up," Sarah said with a big smile.

"I'm counting on you," he replied as he walked out of her cubicle.

Sarah clenched her hands into small fists of excitement. She was determined to get the best scoop and write the best article she had ever written!

Chapter 2

The day of the trip arrived quickly, and Sarah could hardly wait. The sun was shining brightly in the sky, the perfect weather for this kind of trip. She remembered a time when she had to camp out for hours in her car, and it had been pouring. It had been an absolute nightmare, and she was glad that it was very sunny today.

She had already been driving for a while now, and planned on reaching the Clouse estate just around five in the evening. It would give her plenty of time to find the perfect hiding spot, and set up her equipment.

Sarah drove quickly and steadily on the long winding road. As she drove up into the mountains, snow began to cascade down, creating a very picturesque setting. Her two big bags sat in the back, stuffed to the brim. She had packed her best camera, along with a backup one too, wanting to be completely prepared. She was determined to get the best shot possible. If she had to stay at a nearby hotel overnight or something, she was willing to do it, as shown by the changes of clothes she had also packed.

Several large houses lined the road, each more extravagant than the last the more she drove. This was a very popular vacation spot for the rich, and Sarah had never been here before, so she was rather excited to take in the sights. She had read up on the location, and was delighted to find that there was a shopping mall an hour away. She planned on stopping there after completing her assignment to grab some Christmas presents for her friends. The websites online had detailed the special sorts of sweets and other gifts that were unique to the location.

Sarah stared at the road in front of her, and suddenly realized that she had no idea where she was going. She pulled over onto the side, and peered at the open map on the passenger seat beside her. "Okay... I just go straight here... Then turn a right... then another right..." she mumbled absentmindedly to herself for a minute before moving back onto the road. Sarah was a little scared of getting lost, all by herself on the mountain, but she figured as long as she had the map, she would be alright.

She was almost at the house, and she had read in other magazines that their house was the biggest of them all, right at the very top. Sarah had always had a fascination with beautiful mansions. They were always filled with gorgeous art too! She couldn't wait to get a personal look at the house and if it was possible, snap some pictures of the inside.

She reached an intersection rather quickly, and turned to look at the map beside her again as she waited for the light to turn green. There was suddenly the sound of screeching tires, and Sarah looked up, surprised.

Her eyes widened as she saw a car spinning towards her, veering out of control off the road.

It was coming straight at her!

Her heart stopped as she threw her shift into reverse. Was it too late to get out of harm's way?

Her car began to roll backwards, but it wasn't enough to avoid the approaching car altogether.

The other car crashed into the front of her car. Thankfully, Sarah had acted quickly, and the car did not hit her body. If she had not moved, it would have crashed right into the driver's door, a potentially fatal crash.

The airbags deployed with a loud "phish" sound, and her face was enveloped in the white safety bag. She couldn't breathe at first, and adrenaline pumped through her veins as she tried to calm down. *Oh my God... Oh my God...!* she kept thinking as she began to feel rather lightheaded.

A few minutes later, Sarah found her head becoming clear once more. Everything seemed like it was happening in a daze, and she suddenly became aware of a dull pain in her head. She lifted a hand to touch the spot and found that it was wet. Was it blood? She must have hit her head on something when the crash happened.

She heard the car door open.

"Are you okay?" a deep voice murmured quietly. "Hello? Miss?" There was another pause. "Can you hear me?"

"Ah…" Sarah struggled to speak. She suddenly felt hands underneath her body, lifting her, then a wave of fresh air washing over her. "Wha…" She blinked several times, her vision slowly returning to her. "Oh my God!" she gasped as she realized there was a very handsome man staring intently at her.

His piercing blue eyes were wide open, staring deeply into hers. He looked so familiar… And then it hit her. Holding her in his arms was Hamilton Clouse!

"Oh my God!" Sarah cried, surprised.

"Don't move, you're hurt! Let me bring you to my car, it's warm there," he said as he held on to her and walked her over to his luxury car. He opened the door and gently put her down on the seat. "I'm so sorry for crashing into you, I'm not sure what happened and I just lost control. Must be all these slippery roads," he murmured as he straightened up. "Hold on, let me stop the bleeding. I've got some bandages in my first-aid kit. I'll be right back."

He walked over to the rear end of his car and popped open the trunk. He was true to his word, and returned seconds later to Sarah's side. He cleaned her wound and tied the bandage around her head comfortingly. "Is that too tight? Let me know if it hurts. I'm Hamilton, by the way."

"It's just right. And I'm Sarah," Sarah mumbled weakly. "Thank you so much."

"It's really my fault this happened... Please let me take care of the damages. I take full responsibility for this incident," he said. "How about coming back to my place with me? We can exchange insurance information there and have some dinner. And I will make sure that you stay warm, as being cold definitely will be bad for your head. You can call your insurance company at the house."

Sarah realized what a big scoop that could mean for her and Pulse, getting an inside look at Hamilton Clouse's house and life! And Ryan and his new girlfriend were probably going to be there too! Plus, Hamilton was super cute and she kind of wanted to spend more time with him. "That sounds good," she said somewhat weakly.

"How are you feeling?"

"A bit cold," she said honestly as she pulled her jacket around her tightly. The car was warm, but not nearly enough.

"Alright, let me take you home. It's much warmer there. Let me put your seatbelt on… Do you have any valuables in your car? I wouldn't want anything to be stolen!" He reached across her body and his hands gently touched her skin. "My apologies," he said gentlemanly, as he secured the strap across her body.

"Oh, yes, I do have some items that are valuable…" Sarah replied, thinking about how she could go and fetch them. She didn't really want to move, as she was still feeling rather dizzy, but she couldn't just leave her camera there without a plan to get it back.

"How about I'll send someone to get it once we get to my place? You can just give them the keys to the car, and they can bring it all back for you," he said.

"That sounds perfect, thank you so much." Hamilton seemed to think of everything and Sarah really appreciated it. "Could you… get my keys from the ignition?"

"No problem at all. I'll be right back," he said as he left the car and ran over to hers. He returned seconds later, and handed her the keys, which she took gratefully. "Ready to go?" he asked.

"Yes!" Sarah watched him walk around the car and climb into the driver's side. He started the engine.

Hamilton drove smoothly and slowly, trying his utmost best not to jostle the car too much. She was feeling a lot better after he had cleaned her wound, and she was excited that she was going to have a chance to see how he lived, and get an insider's scoop. Terrence would definitely be elated if she did.

They reached the big mansion within ten minutes, and Sarah was completely amazed by how grand the entire house was. "Wow…" she exclaimed as she looked at it from the car window as Hamilton parked. She could probably fit tens of thousands of her apartment in there! So this was what it was like to be truly rich, she thought. Yet Hamilton still was humble, which she liked even more now.

"Still feeling okay?" he said as he pulled open the door and shot her another dazzling smile.

Sarah blushed, giving her cheeks a nice healthy flush of color. "Definitely. Thank you so much."

"Nonsense. It's my pleasure." He laughed as he checked his watch. "Oops, I'm a little late. Let's go inside!" He led her slowly to the front door, where he turned and smiled as he waved to the top right-hand corner, at a little ball. "It's a camera," he explained.

The door opened mere moments later. "Great to see you, Master Hamilton." An older man dressed very neatly in black and white answered the door. Sarah guessed him to be the butler.

"Thank you, Jerry. I've missed you!" Hamilton grinned. "This is Sarah. I bumped into her on the way here." Hamilton took off his jacket, and hung it up nearby in a huge coat closet. Underneath his thick winter jacket, he was wearing a nice warm navy sweater, which looked incredibly good on his tall frame and clung to his slim silhouette. "Oh, could you please also call Steven over? And send someone to Sarah's car to bring it back here."

"Right away, sir. And may I take your coat, Miss Sarah?" Jerry's smile was warm and welcoming.

"Oh, thank you!" Sarah replied gratefully as Jerry took her coat and hung it up next to Hamilton's.

"Do you mind giving your keys to him? Then we can fetch your car," Hamilton reminded her.

"Oh, yes, of course!"

"The rest of the family is already here, and they're in the living room, waiting for you." Jerry bowed before walking away, probably to phone Steven, whoever he was.

"Are you sure I won't be out of place at your family gathering?" Sarah murmured. She didn't want to be the awkward guest there.

"Don't worry about it. I'm sure they won't mind. And I feel bad about crashing into you and causing that cut. I already called for the doctor, don't worry. He'll probably arrive after dinner!"

"Thank you so much," Sarah smiled gratefully. She continued to follow him as they walked into the living room.

"Hello, everyone," Hamilton said as he walked into the room, Sarah in tow.

"Hamilton! Son! Great to see you're finally here." Sarah's eyes widened as she recognized businessman Roger Clouse. He stood up and Hamilton walked towards him and gave him a big hug. "It's been too long, son."

"Hi, Dad." Hamilton grinned. "Merry Christmas!"

"Still got a couple days to go, champ." Roger smiled widely. "Who is this lovely lady?"

Sarah noticed that two other people were also in the room. A lovely, kind-looking blonde woman dressed in a classy beige turtleneck sweater and form-fitting pants sat on the couch that Roger had gotten up from. Sarah assumed this to be Marina Clouse, Roger's wife and Hamilton's mother. From all the news articles written about her, the world saw her as a warm-hearted woman who loved her sons very much, and frequently donated to charities. Marina was a published author, and had taken a break from writing when her sons were born, but now was just beginning to return to the scene.

On the other couch sat the infamous Ryan Clouse, dressed in a thin shirt and dark jeans, looking very casual compared to the rest of his family. She was just wondering where Ryan's girlfriend was, but that question was answered when the loud clacking of heels suddenly started.

"Sorry I took so long, I was having a bit of trouble finding the washroom!" a high-pitched voice trilled, before the body it belonged to came into view. Ryan's girlfriend was exactly what Sarah expected her to look like. With her wavy tresses of thick blonde hair and incredibly revealing V-neck sweater, she certainly made an entrance. She walked to the couch and sat down beside Ryan, kissing him on the cheek not at all subtly. Then she noticed Sarah. "Oh, who's this?"

She immediately gave Sarah the once-over, taking in her somewhat plain winter hoodie and skinny jeans, paired with sneakers. The white bandage on her forehead was also rather obvious and odd-looking. It was her stakeout outfit, and was meant to be completely comfortable, not fashionable. Ryan's girlfriend obviously thought Sarah just had no sense of fashion, and that clearly showed on her face by the catty look she gave Sarah.

"Hamilton was just about to introduce her, Eva," Roger said. Eva didn't even bother to introduce herself.

"Yes! This is Sarah. I accidentally drove into her car today, and since it's my fault, I want her to stay here until Steven can check her injuries and our mechanic can get her car going again," Hamilton said with a gentle smile.

Roger laughed. "Alright, welcome, Sarah! I'm sorry about Hamilton's driving skills," he joked as Marina also giggled.

"Hello! Nice to meet you." Sarah smiled warmly at everyone.

"Enjoy yourself! We should be having dinner in about an hour or so, I do hope you'll join us. In the meantime… It's a big house, Hamilton, why don't you give her a tour?"

"Sounds good. Let's go?" Hamilton said to Sarah.

"Sure!" Sarah replied.

"We'll see you guys at dinner then!" Hamilton said to the rest of the room. "Are you feeling well enough for a tour?" he said to Sarah, gesturing at her head. "I tied it up the best I could but I'm not a doctor, so I don't want to put any unnecessary stress on you before he arrives."

Sarah grinned bravely. "I'll be okay!" She wanted to see the rest of the house, as it could make good material for her article. She had already memorized what Eva was wearing, and what brand it was from too. Readers loved to see pictures and copy what celebrities wore, so she made a mental note to snap some pictures of it later.

"Alright, let's go then! It's a big house, so we'd better start now." Hamilton laughed heartily. He had a captivating laugh that Sarah found to be quite infectious, and before long, the two were strolling through the house looking at the architecture and artwork, laughing like crazy.

Hamilton was incredibly down-to-earth, and the more Sarah talked to him, the more she liked him. She knew that she wasn't supposed to be here flirting, but instead gathering information. However, she genuinely wanted to know more about this handsome businessman. The more she learned, the more interested she was in him.

Hamilton knew about all sorts of interesting things, and he had unique views on all sorts of topics. One thing she realized he was very passionate about was animals. In particular, otters. "What do you like most about otters?" Sarah asked as they rounded the corner, heading into a room full of coins. Hamilton had previously explained that Roger had a hobby of collecting rare coins from all over the world, and various other rooms were filled with other weird collections.

"It's a bit embarrassing to say this…" Hamilton said. "But I think it's absolutely adorable when they hold hands. You know, when they sleep? I've actually got a picture of it on my phone."

Sarah laughed, slightly amazed. She never would have guessed that Hamilton would have such a soft spot for animals. In the interviews he gave, all the journalists only asked him about things related to business, so if she wrote an article with new facts about his personal life, that would definitely make it a better read.

While she had been looking at the coins, Hamilton had pulled out his phone and had really clicked into the photo. "Here, look!" he said as he showed her the truly cute otters holding paws as they drifted on the water.

"This is so cute!" Sarah giggled as Hamilton swiped to the left to reveal even more photos. She wasn't just talking about the otters; this side of Hamilton was definitely cute too. He always seemed so indifferent in interviews, so this was a welcome change. Plus, she could barely keep her eyes off him. He was incredibly handsome, and she hoped she wasn't being too obvious about it.

"Shall we move on to the next room?" He grinned.

"Yeah, sure!" she said as she followed him out onto the corridor. Looking down the nearby stairs, she noticed that Eva and Ryan were relaxing on the large sofas. Eva turned her head immediately as Sarah looked down, giving her the impression that Eva had previously been staring at her. It was odd, but Sarah shrugged it off. She had done nothing wrong, and there would be no reason why Eva would dislike her.

"Oh, you two! This is perfect timing!" Marina called from the bottom floor. "Dinner will be served shortly, why don't you join us in the dining room?"

"Yes, we'll come down, thank you, Mother!" Hamilton responded.

"Oh, it's dinnertime already? Time sped by fast!" Sarah checked her watch to find that it was seven o'clock. The tour of the house had been so interesting, she hadn't even noticed how long it was. She really enjoyed spending time with Hamilton, and a part of her wished that it could last longer. But it was alright. She hoped that she would be able to spend some more time with him after dinner.

"I'm glad you enjoyed the 'tour.' I'm not a very good tour guide…" He laughed as they walked towards the long staircase to the first floor.

"No, you are! It was fun. And this house is like a museum! So many rare items everywhere. This place is huge, too. It's a bit overwhelming." Sarah giggled as they made their way down towards the dining room.

"Yeah… It takes some getting used to, definitely," he agreed as they reached the bottom of the stairs. "My father keeps some of his smaller collections here, and at our main house there are mostly his collections of rare furniture."

Jerry walked out and smiled at the pair warmly. "Miss Sarah, your belongings have been fetched from your car. Here are your keys." He handed the keys back to her politely. "They're in the living room right now, beside the big couch on the left. Your car is in the garage! It should be ready to run again soon."

"Thank you so much!" Sarah gushed as she took the keys and slid them into her pocket. Jerry definitely would not have opened the bags, so her journalist secret was safe. She didn't want the family to find out that she was here to gain information for her article! They would be greatly offended by that.

"Let's go for dinner. Thank you, Jerry, please let me know when Steven arrives later," Hamilton said. Hamilton and Sarah walked towards the dining room once again.

"Ah, Hamilton, there you are!" Roger exclaimed loudly as the two walked through the door to the giant dining room. "I was beginning to think you didn't want to eat with us!"

Sarah was definitely surprised as she walked into the dining room. It was absolutely huge! There was a gorgeous chandelier hanging from the ceiling, and bunches of flowers in the middle of the table. The food smelled delicious, and it definitely made Sarah feel hungry.

Everyone was already sitting around the table, waiting for them.

"Hello, you two!" Marina smiled warmly. "How was the tour?"

"Oh, it was lovely! The house is amazing, I especially liked the different collections," Sarah gushed as Hamilton pulled out the chair for her. "Thank you."

"I'm glad you enjoyed it! Tonight Anne, the cook, is making one of her signature dishes. Italian chicken parmesan pasta with Anne's self-made sauce. It's fantastic, you really don't want to miss it!" Marina laughed as she sipped some of her red wine.

True to Marina's word, Anne's chicken parmesan was definitely incredibly delicious. The rest of the dinner was also delightful, with quick and easy conversation with everyone, except Eva, who just ate her dinner coolly as she stared down at her plate. Marina and Roger were so wonderfully inviting, and Sarah was really liking the whole atmosphere.

Especially Hamilton.

He never failed to make her laugh with one of his many humorous remarks and jokes, and she liked the fact that his jokes were classy ones. She had once been on a blind date where the man did nothing but make fart jokes all night long! Sarah thought that was simply immature and ridiculous.

It wasn't long before the chicken parmesan was all finished, and Sarah was feeling quite satisfied. Almost everyone had finished theirs completely, with the exception of Eva, who claimed she was "watching her weight."

"Are you ready for dessert?" Marina smiled fondly.

"Oh, I'm so full, I don't think I could eat another bite!" Sarah laughed as she drank some water from her glass.

"Try some! You won't regret it." Just as Marina said this, two butlers swept in with the dessert, and placed one in front of each person. "It's my favorite, apple crumble pie with ice cream on top."

As full as she was, Sarah had to admit, it looked incredibly delicious. So she picked up her fork and took a bite. Wow! It melted in her mouth, a combination of cold and hot that was just heavenly tasting. She wondered if the Clouses ate luxurious food like this every day, and she felt somewhat envious of that.

Eva only ate a tiny bit of the pie, and gave the rest to Ryan, who eagerly ate it for her. Eva seemed to Sarah like a very typical, somewhat stereotypical kind of girl who watched her weight very carefully, always dressed to the nines, judged others by their appearance, and always felt like she had to be the star of the show. But Ryan looked like he was totally in love with her, and she always acted sweet to Marina and Roger.

Eva raised her eyes and looked at Hamilton, who promptly looked away as soon as he saw her. Sarah noticed the tension between the two almost immediately, and wondered if it was because he didn't like her, or if she had done something to offend him in the past. If she could find out, that would be an interesting point for her article.

"Master Hamilton, Dr. Tyre, Steven, has arrived and is waiting in the living room," Jerry said, interrupting Sarah's thoughts.

"Oh, yes, thank you, Jerry. Mother, we'll be going to see Steven now, if that's alright," Hamilton said as he smiled at Sarah.

"No problem at all. I'll see you later!" Marina grinned warmly.

"Let's go," Hamilton said as he stood up, and Sarah did the same.

"Okay!"

They walked out of the dining room into the living room, where a handsome man dressed in a nice sweater sat. As soon as he saw Hamilton, he stood up and they shook hands in a rather familiar manner. "Hi, Hamilton. What's going on?"

"It's not me, actually, it's Sarah here," Hamilton said as he gently led Sarah to walk until she was in front of him. "The road was slippery today, and I crashed into her car. She hit her head a little, and I had my first-aid kit, so I bandaged her up. I want to be sure that there isn't any more serious damage, so I had Jerry call you. So sorry if I bothered you in the middle of your vacation."

"Oh, don't worry about it. It is no problem for such a great friend," Steven said as he pulled out a black doctor's bag and produced from it a stethoscope and all kinds of other medical equipment she didn't know the names of.

"How is Sophie? I haven't seen her in quite some time," Hamilton asked.

The whole exchange sounded like something out of a formal greeting book, and it made Sarah laugh a little in her head.

"Sophie is doing well! We're actually expecting a second child! A boy. We just found out the news a week ago, so it's all very exciting." Steven grinned as he stuck the stethoscope into his ears. "Take deep breaths in and out for me, please," he said to Sarah, who obeyed.

"Oh wow, that's fantastic. I love children." Hamilton smiled. Sarah was struck with a thought that Hamilton seemed like he'd make a pretty good father.

Sarah breathed as Steven instructed, and half a minute later, Steven made his verdict. "Your heart sounds healthy, which is good. Does any part of your arms or body hurt? Were any of them caught in the car during the crash?"

"I don't think so. I can move them easily, and I've had no trouble walking," Sarah answered promptly. "It's just my head is starting to ache again… just a little." She touched her head gingerly, careful not to cause any more pain.

"Let me take a look at the wound…" Steven said gently as he removed the bandage. "Well, you did an excellent job stopping the bleeding, Hamilton. It actually helped a lot, and the wound looks pretty clean. It looks like just a cut, and though it should hurt for the next little while, it should definitely heal up nicely. I don't see any signs of a concussion. Just keep it clean, and if you feel any pain, over-the-counter medicine should be fine for that," he said in a very smart manner as he removed his stethoscope.

"That's good to hear." Sarah breathed a sigh of relief.

"I have some medicine, don't worry," Hamilton offered helpfully. His smile was incredibly calming, though she didn't know why.

"You should rest for these next few days. Getting sleep helps with almost every condition, and helps prevent further damage." Steven smiled as he took out some new bandaging and some sanitizing equipment. "I'm just going to clean the wound some more, to make sure that it won't become infected, and will put on some new dressing."

Sarah nodded. "Thank you so much."

"No problem... Now it'll sting a little when I clean the wound..." Steven warned.

Sarah didn't have a particularly high tolerance for pain, and she winced a little when the doctor worked on her forehead. Hamilton noticed, and he put a comforting hand on hers. His hand was so warm, and she found that she really liked the feeling of their hands pressed together.

The entire process didn't take long, less than eight minutes. This doctor was skilled, and Sarah was grateful that Hamilton had called him.

"Alright, all finished!" Steven exclaimed as he cleaned up and packed up his bag once more. "How do you feel, Sarah?"

"Great. Thank you!" Sarah stood up and shook Steven's hand before sitting down onto the couch once more. It was actually an extremely comfortable plush piece of furniture, and she felt like she could sit there forever.

Hamilton and Steven exchanged small talk, before Steven received a call and had to go. It was probably from his wife, Sophie. "Thanks for coming by,

Steven. Let's get together some time for some golf, or perhaps dinner," Hamilton said with a smile.

"Sounds good to me."

"I can show you out, Dr. Tyre," Jerry said as he reappeared, and he led Steven away.

Hamilton then turned his attention to Sarah, who was still sitting on the couch. "I'm glad there was no big damage. But I'm sorry there had to be any damage at all. It's a shame that there has to be a wound on such a pretty face," he said as he sat down too, and stared at her in the eyes. For some reason, that made her flush a pretty pink, which he thought was adorable.

She realized that he had noticed her blush. "Must be hot in here…" she mumbled, trying to cover up her embarrassment. She was never good at taking compliments, and it sounded so wonderful coming from him.

"So do you have family near here? Is that why you were driving all the way here so close to the holidays?" Hamilton asked in a friendly manner as he relaxed on the sofa.

He looked quite gorgeous as he sank back into the luxurious seats. His dark chocolate tresses, lightly combed to the side, looked effortless. Sarah found herself wanting to run her fingers through that fine mane, and stare forever into those blue eyes, so blue that they reminded her of the never-ending ocean. She liked the way he dressed, it was mature and very fashionable.

"Oh, no… I don't actually have any plans for the holidays…" Sarah said honestly. She usually spent the holidays with her best friend Victoria, but Victoria had been studying and working abroad in Japan since September, so they could only stay in touch using voice and video chat. "I was just planning on staying home, maybe doing a little shopping, perhaps going out to a restaurant… Nothing really special." She realized her small holiday plans must have sounded quite boring and plain to Hamilton, who probably went skiing in Switzerland or sunbathing on the sunny beaches of Miami with his family every year. Sarah had enjoyed reading about the Clouses and their extravagant vacations in the tabloids.

"Well… Since you're not doing anything… And Steven did say you should definitely get some rest… Would you like to stay here and celebrate the holidays with us?" Hamilton said considerately. He wasn't doing it out of pity; he truly wanted to spend more time with her, as the afternoon they had spent together had been rather wonderful and he wanted to continue that. Sarah was such a smart, funny girl that he couldn't help but feel like he wanted to get to know her better.

It was an incredibly generous offer, and Sarah considered it seriously. It would be an even better opportunity to snap pictures and gain information for the article, and perhaps gain more information about Eva and Ryan's relationship, though Eva didn't seem to like her much. Plus, Hamilton was very attractive, and Sarah really wanted to get to know him better. But she knew that it would be kind of weird for her to stay with them, since they had just met. "Um... I don't know. I don't want to intrude, as Christmas is a family holiday, and I don't want to make you all feel uncomfortable since I'm basically a stranger," Sarah said reasonably.

"No problem! My mother always says the more the merrier. And my father and Ryan definitely won't mind. I could tell, they really liked you tonight!" Hamilton grinned.

"Alright... I guess I'll stay then."

Hamilton smiled back at her. "Great. I'm sure we have several guest rooms ready to be used. Shall we bring your bags up to a room together?" he offered as he stood up.

"Oh, thank you. Yes please," Sarah said as she followed him to the bigger couch, where her bags lay. He picked up two of them easily, leaving her the small light one to bring up. She picked it up easily, and they marched up the stairs.

"That's my room, there." Hamilton pointed at the door on the very left of the hallway. "Now I think the rooms next to it are vacant, let me just double-check." He opened the door right beside his, and peered inside. "Perfect. Come take a look," he said as he walked into the room.

"Oh my..." Sarah gasped as she stepped into the room after him. The room was every bit as luxurious as the rest of the house. Huge glass doors lined half of a wall, giving a fantastic view of the snowy atmosphere. It was an amazing view, and the doors opened to allow one to step out onto the balcony.

The sky was already dark, and it was just barely snowing. Sarah loved snow! She loved the way it felt on her skin, the way it slowly fell from the sky like little drops of heaven and the way each snowflake melted on her tongue. She longed to go out onto the balcony and take in the view, but she decided that she would do that later.

"This is amazing," Sarah said, turning towards Hamilton.

"I'll take that as a yes," Hamilton replied happily. "Now, you can use this room however you want, but I only ask that you try not to damage any of the paintings or decorations, as some of them are part of my mother's collection. Not that I think you would."

"Of course, I'll definitely take good care of it. Don't worry!"

"Perfect. I'll leave you to unpack now, but if you need anything, I'll just be next door." He pointed to the left before smiling once more as he exited the room, closing the door behind him.

Sarah was filled with glee as she jumped onto the huge king-sized bed with the biggest grin on her face. She had *never* stayed in such a beautiful place like this. This room could even give some five-star hotel rooms a run for their money! Sarah recognized some of the art hanging as the work of well-known painters. Undoubtedly, they were worth a lot of money.

As Sarah looked around the room as she lay on the bed, she realized that the bed's mattress was so unbelievably soft. Sarah felt like she was going to fall asleep right away. But she couldn't.

She had work to do.

Springing to life once more, Sarah walked over to her bags, and pulled out her camera. It would be nice to get some pictures of the room, and maybe of some of the art too. She snapped a couple pictures, testing it out. Then she realized that it would probably be a good idea to call Terrence to tell him of her incredible luck. There was no doubt in her mind that he would be pleased.

Sarah had Terrence's personal cell number, and she only had to wait three seconds before Terrence picked up. "Terrence here," he said as if he were in a hurry. He always sounded like that on the phone, probably because he actually was always busy.

"Hi, it's Sarah," she said as she sank down onto a plush armchair. "I have good news. Guess where I am right now."

"Doing your job, outside the Clouses' home, hopefully taking many pictures of them?"

"I'm *in* the Clouse home right now!" Sarah exclaimed excitedly.

"Please tell me you didn't break and enter," Terrence said with a hint of humor in his voice.

"No, no, see, what happened was that Hamilton Clouse's car bumped into mine so he brought me back to his place, and he just asked me to stay and spend Christmas with them for the next few days!"

There was silence for a bit as Terrence processed what she had said. "Oh God, that's so perfect. It'll be the perfect opportunity for picture taking and fact gathering. This article could be front cover material! Yes, Sarah, thank God for your luck! A Christmas miracle! This could really launch our magazine's popularity even higher! Please tell me you said yes."

"Of course I said yes! And I met Ryan's new girlfriend. Her name is Eva. She doesn't seem very friendly though… I'll try and get some pictures of them together," Sarah said as she played with her camera's settings, pressing her ear to her shoulder to keep her phone there so she could multitask.

"Great. Outstanding job, Sarah. Keep me updated, and don't forget to work on the article too. I've got to go now, but I'll definitely talk to you later!" There was a click at the other end as Terrence hung up.

Sarah grinned as she snapped another picture of the view outside. She was actually somewhat tired, so she decided that she would just take a small nap, for an hour or so, and wake up later to do some work on her article. She set a small alarm on her phone within a minute.

Then Sarah opened one of her bags and rifled through it, looking for her sleepwear. She changed into her loose red-and-white sleep top and matching capris. She looked very cute, and felt rather warm. The house was already pretty well heated, and Sarah had no worries about being cold there. She crawled underneath the heavy covers after turning off the lights, and almost immediately, drifted off into sleep.

***

Sarah woke some time later, blinking rapidly in a room full of darkness. For a moment, she forgot where she was, until she felt the plush mattress and thick covers. *Right... I'm at Hamilton's mansion,* she thought as she sat up sleepily, rubbing her eyes.

She reached blindly for her phone, and after she found it, she unlocked it. The bright glare of the screen made her wince, as she waited for her auto-brightening screen to adjust to the dark. "Oh, damn, it's midnight already! I must have slept through my alarm!" Sarah's mouth twisted in a grimace. Her throat was feeling quite dry, as she had just woken up. "I could really use some of that fresh spring water we had at dinner," she murmured.

She slipped out of bed. Sarah hoped that everyone was already asleep, and no one would catch her in her rather embarrassing casual pajamas that consisted of loose black capris and a tank top. It wouldn't be too hard to find a glass and fill it up with some water in the kitchen.

Sarah walked as softly as she could down the stairs, using her phone's flashlight as a guide. She managed to find the kitchen, thanks to Hamilton's grand tour of the house earlier. After getting the drink, she quickly made her way back to her room with an extra glass full just in case she got thirsty later. As she climbed the stairs, her phone's flashlight suddenly went out. "Uh-oh. Did the battery run out?" she whispered.

She continued forwards, until suddenly, she bumped into something hard. "Oh!" she exclaimed as quietly as she could. She hoped the water didn't spill. And who had she hit?

"We must stop meeting like this," came a deep voice that sent chills down her spine. Hamilton!

"Oh, God, I'm sorry," Sarah said as she blushed.

"What are you still doing awake?" Hamilton asked as he pulled out his own phone and turned on the flashlight feature, casting a bright glow on their faces.

"I was just getting some water. Then my phone's flashlight died! And I don't really like the dark, but I don't know where the lights are," Sarah explained.

"Oh!" Hamilton laughed a little, quietly. "Let me take you to your room."

"Thank you so much."

"Let's go. Careful, it's pretty dark, try not to bump into anything. I want you to be safe and sound," Hamilton murmured sweetly. "Ah, here we are."

Hamilton opened the door to her room, and flipped a switch. All of the lights flashed on, and Sarah felt relieved to be able to see properly again. It turned out her phone had run out of battery, which was why the flashlight had turned off earlier. "So why were you roaming the halls?" Sarah asked. Perhaps Hamilton had insomnia! That would be an interesting tidbit to put into her article.

"For some reason, I couldn't sleep tonight. I had just finished the new Stephen King novel, and reading before bed usually helps me sleep. So I thought about going downstairs to maybe grab a small bite to eat and a nice cup of hot cocoa. It's one of my favorite drinks, though it's a little childish..." Hamilton laughed sheepishly.

"Hot cocoa sounds a lot better than this plain old water." Sarah gestured to the cup of water she was holding in her hand.

"I can go downstairs and make us some cups of cocoa. And perhaps some light snacks? That is, if you're in the mood for it," Hamilton offered as Sarah set her glass of water down onto the nightstand.

"That actually sounds amazing. I haven't had hot cocoa since, well... forever!" Sarah laughed quietly.

"I'll get right on it then. I should be done in like... ten minutes. Can you stay awake that long?" There was a twinkle in his eyes as he said it, which Sarah thought was incredibly adorable. "I promise I'll be as fast as I can."

"I'll be waiting!" Sarah grinned as she took a seat on one of the comfy armchairs. Hamilton gave her one last smile before pulling open the door and heading out. Sarah couldn't help but smile back, feeling her cheeks slightly turning pink.

True to his word, Hamilton returned just shy of ten minutes later, holding two cups full of piping hot brown liquid. Small marshmallows floated on the top, rapidly melting in the cocoa. "Here. I also brought a pack of chocolate chip cookies," he said as he placed the two cups onto the coffee table and pulled a white package out from the pocket of his pajama bottoms.

He still looked incredibly handsome even dressed in such casual sleepwear. His loose button- up top hung off his broad shoulders perfectly, as if it were custom-made. Sarah found herself checking him out, and quickly realized that she was probably being unsubtle. A tiny bit of blush crept its way onto her face. Hamilton noticed, and smiled. Sarah grabbed a mug and watched as Hamilton opened the pack of cookies.

She felt so relaxed here in this room, with him. She couldn't remember the last time she had felt so open. It was as if all her cares had vanished.

"Tell me about yourself, Sarah," Hamilton said after he took a sip of the delicious cocoa. "I want to know more about you."

"About me? Oh… There's nothing interesting about me," Sarah said modestly. She didn't want to talk about her job, of course, but it looked like Hamilton wasn't going to give up.

"I'm sure you're *very* interesting, Sarah! Tell me anything." He was genuinely curious about her, and she could tell that he wasn't just making small talk.

"Alright, fine. Where should I begin?"

"Well, at the beginning, of course!"

Chapter 3

Over the course of the next three days, Sarah and Hamilton talked for hours on end in the morning, over lunch, and into the wee hours of the evening. They were addicted to each other. Sarah found Hamilton so interesting and so fun to be around. Though he loved to work, he also had many interesting hobbies, like horseback riding, which he talked passionately about. Hamilton felt the same about Sarah. She was witty and kind of mysterious, which only made him more curious.

Sarah wasn't sure how to describe the feelings she felt for Hamilton.

Whenever she saw him, there was this raw, passionate urge to just kiss him, and the need to just be with him. It felt like more than a crush, yet Sarah was too afraid to call it love. Was it possible to fall in love in only three days?

But it was true that it was like nothing she had ever experienced before. She didn't know if he felt the same, and knew it would be awkward if he didn't. But she couldn't help but feel that something, a connection perhaps, was happening between them, and she hoped that he felt it too.

Sarah stood on the balcony, contemplating these thoughts. She gazed out at the spectacular view of the snowy land, trying to make sense of her feelings. Sarah knew that she couldn't stay in this winter vacation-of-sorts forever. After Christmas, she had to leave. Just thinking about it made her feel rather sad.

Sarah sighed as she walked back into her room, and stripped off her coat.

She wanted to tell Hamilton her feelings, but was scared of rejection. After all, he was such an eligible bachelor, she was sure he had women throwing themselves at him all the time. With all the Clouses' magazine features, Hamilton was definitely at least somewhat known for his good looks as well as his smarts. Why would he be interested in her?

Sarah picked up her camera from its previous spot in the nightstand drawer, and looked through the photos she had taken. She had managed to get many pictures of Eva and Ryan, without them finding out. Marina had also hinted that Ryan was going to propose tonight, which Sarah knew she just had to get pictures of. She had mastered the art of taking stealthy photos with her phone, and had the feeling that she was going to be utilizing that skill a lot tonight.

She had also completed two drafts of her article for Pulse, and planned on looking it over once more before sending it to Terrence for his critique. She knew he would be pleased, especially with the photos.

Hamilton was working next door, and Sarah didn't want to bother him, though she did want to talk to him. He always had something interesting to say, and watching him laugh was so exhilarating; the way he threw his head back and the way his blue eyes lit up was so addicting to watch.

Sarah caught herself thinking about Hamilton again, and found that her heart was actually beating rather loudly and quickly. "That can't be good," she mumbled to herself as she pressed a hand against her chest. She tried to put him out of her mind. But it was hard.

Knock, knock!

Two short knocks came on the door. Sarah's heart skipped a beat. That's how Hamilton usually knocked, and now she was very excited to see him. "Come in!" Sarah said as she put her camera away.

"Hi, Sarah," Hamilton's now very familiar voice called as he opened the door. "Ready for dinner? We're having steak tonight! Anna just loves Christmas so even the day *before* Christmas Eve, today, she makes food that is extra special; you don't want to miss it!"

"Oh, is it that time already? I'm coming, just give me a second!" Sarah grinned. "Steak sounds delicious."

Hamilton stepped inside. "I'll wait for you."

Sarah walked to the connected bathroom, ran a brush quickly through her blonde locks, and checked herself out in the mirror to make sure that she looked presentable. She headed out of the washroom, grabbed her smartphone, and then walked until she was beside Hamilton. "Let's go?"

"Let's."

Hamilton opened the door for her and the two walked steadily until they reached the dining room. Someone had decorated it in a very Christmas-y fashion, with red and green decorations everywhere. Sarah smiled, feeling the abundance of Christmas spirit. She didn't notice, but Hamilton was looking at her with a soft look in his eyes.

The dinner was fantastic, courtesy of Anne. After wonderfully filling steaks, the entire family headed into the living room for some wine. Eva was already on her second glass, and was laughing very loudly at all the jokes Ryan made.

"Now, everyone, listen," Ryan said as he stood up. "I have something to say."

"What is it, son?" Roger said with a grin, as if he already knew what Ryan was going to say.

Ryan turned his attention towards Eva, who was dressed in a tight white sweater dress that was much too short to be anywhere near modest. Sarah wondered if her legs were cold at all. "Eva…" Ryan started as he sank down onto one knee. "Eva, I love you so much."

Eva reacted in a very typical manner, immediately putting both hands over her mouth as she opened her eyes so wide they looked like saucers. "Oh my God, Ryan!" she exclaimed loudly. She didn't look actually surprised, something that Sarah noticed and thought was somewhat odd. Nonetheless, she brought out her phone and subtly took several photos.

"I want to be with you forever. And I know you feel the same way about me," he said as he pulled out a small velvet ring box and opened it. "Will you marry me?"

"Yes!" Eva squealed as she let Ryan put the ring on her finger. She embraced him tightly, and they kissed noisily.

"Oh, how sweet," Marina said, looking at Roger proudly. "We raised him well."

"We sure did, Mari," Roger replied as he squeezed Marina's hand in a fond manner.

Sarah smiled at the happy scene unfolding in front of her. Eva had stopped hugging Ryan and was now admiring the huge rock on her ring. It certainly was very big and attention-grabbing; it must have cost him a fortune.

Sarah zoomed in and snapped the best picture that she could of the gorgeous piece of jewelry. That picture would definitely be a decisive one.

They celebrated with some more wine, and with Eva recounting the events of when she first met Ryan. There was a nice, happy atmosphere in the whole room, and Sarah thought with a smile that this was what families should be like. Sarah was an only child. Her father had died when she was young, and her mother more recently. Hamilton, though, was curiously calm and rather indifferent about the whole thing, and Sarah wondered why he wasn't acting very happy for his brother.

Eventually, the celebrations ended and Sarah was just about to head upstairs to inspect her photos when a hand on her wrist stopped her right at the stairs. "Sarah," Hamilton said as she whirled around.

"Hi, Hamilton." Her heart melted when she saw him standing there, smiling at her. Wow, his smile was really something. She wasn't sure how he did it, but it seemed to have some sort of magic.

"I don't really want to turn in for the night just yet… Would you join me in the sitting room for some cocoa?" The sitting room was usually used for Roger's business associates, when he brought them up to the mansion to try and get them to sign on a deal. It was a cozy room with a fireplace, for Roger believed that was the best environment for someone to feel the safest and to make them more open.

"That sounds nice."

"I'll meet you there in five minutes. And I'll bring some cookies too." Hamilton winked playfully before speeding away to the kitchen.

Sarah made her way to the sitting room, and sat down on one of the two armchairs, sinking immediately into the plush seat. Oh God, she was so nervous to spend time with Hamilton. She had finally admitted to herself that yes, she was falling for him, and falling hard. But that new decision brought with it a whole new bunch of confusion. Was it too fast for these feelings?

"Hey, here you go," Hamilton called as he walked in and handed her the cup of cocoa, before closing the door behind him.

The fireplace was already roaring, and made the room quite warm in addition to casting a nice glow all around. It was all very romantic, and Sarah became suddenly much too aware of that fact. "So, great news about Ryan and Eva, eh?" she started, not sure what to say. Then she remembered how stoic Hamilton had looked earlier, and kind of regretted asking the question.

"Yeah… I guess," he answered nonchalantly.

The inner journalist within her was curious, so she pressed him on it. "Is something wrong?"

"Oh, it's nothing big. It's just…" He hesitated, not sure if he should tell her or not. But he felt that he could trust her so he decided to. "I used to date Eva. We kept our relationship secret. Even now, my family knows nothing about it. She cheated on me with Ryan, and when I told her that I would tell my brother, because it was the right thing to do, she threatened to tell lies that I raped her. Plus I know how much it would really hurt Ryan," Hamilton explained. "I tried to tell him that Eva wasn't a good match for him, but he being himself, he just thought I was jealous."

Sarah noticed what looked to be a flicker of pain in his eyes as he talked. She suddenly felt rather mad at Eva. How could she betray Hamilton like that? Sarah hadn't liked Eva very much from the get-go, but she liked Eva even less now. Was Eva even in love with Ryan? She did look like she was faking the surprise of the proposal… Sarah made a mental note to find out later. For now, she was focusing on Hamilton.

"I'm so sorry that had to happen to you, Hamilton. It should never happen to anyone. I've been cheated on before too… It really hurts." Sarah placed a hand on Hamilton's arm comfortingly, as she stared into his eyes. Unconsciously, she was leaning in towards him. She wanted to be closer; she wanted to help him heal from the pain.

Hamilton's face was expressionless as he stared back at her. She couldn't tell what he was thinking at all, until he shifted forwards too, and their lips touched.

Sarah was very, very surprised at first when she felt the soft touch of his supple lips press onto hers. Her eyes closed instinctively as she leaned into the kiss even further, wanting to remember this moment forever. Good God, Hamilton was a fantastic kisser.

When he pulled away moments later, Sarah found herself breathless. Her chest lifted up and down as she smiled softly to herself. She thought it was only in the movies that time seemed to stop when the main characters kissed, but this time, it had actually happened.

"I'm sorry, Sarah. That was highly inappropriate of me. I apologize if you don't feel the same way towards me," Hamilton said maturely. "You just looked so... irresistible."

She loved the way he said her name, the way it rumbled off his tongue. "A-and how do you feel towards me?" Sarah stuttered, her heart racing. She was aware that her hands were slightly trembling, for she was so incredibly excited. What was he going to say?

"Well, Sarah... I'm not sure I can say it. I'm sure you'll think that I'm crazy if I tell you," Hamilton said as he raised a hand to his lips in contemplation.

"Tell me!" she goaded him softly.

"I... I think I'm beginning to fall in love with you."

Sarah's heart felt like it was going to explode with happiness.

"I know it sounds ridiculous. I'm actually terrifyingly aware of that fact. But I've never felt anything this strong for anyone I've ever dated. And I know we're not even dating, and now I feel silly for telling you," Hamilton said quickly, as if he were nervous too.

"Hamilton... These past few days have been amazing. I want to spend all my time with you. Just seeing you makes my heart race and my breath hitch. I'd love nothing more than to be with you. I just never thought it was possible for you to like me." Sarah decided that being honest was the best course of action.

"God, Sarah, you make me just want to kiss you," Hamilton murmured as he set his mug on the table. Sarah did the same.

"Then kiss me." Sarah had never been so bold before, and to tell the truth, she was absolutely terrified. She wasn't sure what was going to happen, but she knew that Hamilton was falling for her too, and that was all she needed to know.

Hamilton stood up and offered her his hand. She took it, and he pulled her up, wrapping an arm around her waist as he did. Their anxious mouths touched once more in an electrically charged moment.

It just felt so right for Sarah to be in Hamilton's arms. She relaxed as she wrapped her hands around his neck, their breaths mixing as they kissed so passionately it took Sarah's breath away. When they finally pulled away, seconds later, they were both gasping for air.

"Wow…" Sarah murmured quietly. She was speechless and in complete awe. That kiss confirmed that his feelings for her were real, and it was definitely surprising to say the least. Now she knew that she was in love with him too, and it was so frightfully exciting.

"Wow indeed," he mirrored.

They just stood and stared at each other, both of them not sure what to say. Sarah felt an overwhelming joy in her heart that she just couldn't put into words. She collapsed into the armchair, biting her lip simultaneously. She was smiling, and so was he.

Under the light from the fireplace, Hamilton thought Sarah looked quite beautiful, and he told her so, which made her blush. "Sarah, it would be my pleasure to take you out on a proper date. I'd really like to spend some more time with you, if you can maybe stay at the mansion for a little while longer?"

Sarah was sure Terrence would allow her to stay a while longer, especially since now she had gotten pictures of the proposal. She intended on calling him later, to let him know and to ask his permission. But for now... She wanted to enjoy every moment she had with Hamilton.

His eyes sparkled as he talked with an animated gaiety, his hands fluttering, a habit that she thought was quite endearing. She could listen to him talk for hours, and that's exactly what she did. After a while, all the hot cocoa had been finished, and the fire was dying, but they were still so wide awake and excited.

When they finally said good night, sealing it with a passionate kiss, it was very late. Sarah decided that it would not be wise to wake Terrence, so she would call him tomorrow to let him know of the good news. She jumped onto her bed immediately with a big smile on her face. Hamilton had asked for her number too.

Right as she was about to sleep, she realized that she had a text waiting for her, from an unknown number. She opened it, and realized it was from Hamilton.

Hope you sleep well. I know I will (pardon my being cliché), because I'll be thinking of you. Good night, beautiful. Hamilton.

Sarah let out a girly giggle. She was quite certain she was blushing again. It was a good feeling. She loved the beginning of a relationship, where everything was perfect and she saw the world through rose-tinted glasses. It was an addicting feeling, and she hoped that there would be many more of these perfect days in her future.

Chapter 4

"Hello?" Terrence picked up quickly, like usual. Sarah had decided to call him early in the morning, and was sure he was awake. He was an early riser, as he liked to go for a run while the streets were quiet.

"Hey, it's me. I have good news," Sarah said as she lay down on the bed, staring up at the reddish canopy above her.

"Do tell," Terrence said with delight laced in his tone.

"Ryan proposed last night to Eva! I've got pictures of the actual proposal, and I'll try and get some more. I'm also very close to finishing the article completely. I'll send you it when I'm done."

"That sounds good. I look forward to it, Sarah! Keep up the good work. You're definitely working your way towards a promotion, it all depends on the article! Alright, I have to run, bye!" he replied happily, before hanging up.

She got up, and washed her face down with some cool water, waking herself up. She wanted to spend some more time with Hamilton today. Just as she finished changing, two short knocks came at her door. "Sarah?" Hamilton's voice called. "Are you in there?"

"Yeah, I am!" Sarah opened the door to see Hamilton's handsome face. He was already dressed formally in a suit. "Mmm... You look formal," she commented after he pressed his lips to hers in a mind-numbing kiss.

"Yes... Unfortunately I've got a tiny business crisis I have to sort out at the main office, back in the city so I will be away for the most of the day." Hamilton frowned as he pulled Sarah into his arms, her soft sweater pressing against him. "I really wanted to spend the day with you but I just got the call about the emergency."

Sarah's face fell. "Aw." Her lips twisted into a small, cute pout.

"But... Don't worry! I definitely don't want to leave you without anything to do. My mother was saying earlier that she was going to go into town, and do some shopping. She always enjoys the holiday atmosphere. Why don't you go with her?" Hamilton said as they descended the stairs, his arm swung lightly around her shoulders.

"That sounds like a pretty good idea." Sarah grinned. She actually quite liked Marina, and would be delighted to spend more time with her. Especially if she wanted to have a future with Hamilton.

"We should go ask her if she minds having a little company, though I don't think she will. She should be in the dining room, for breakfast," Hamilton said as they walked into the dining room, and true to his prediction, she was there. A plain white bowl sat in front of her, filled with fruit and yogurt, sprinkled with what appeared to be cereal. It looked great, and very healthy. Marina was very health conscious, and Sarah liked that about her. It was the reason she still looked so young.

"Oh, hello, Hamilton, Sarah." She noticed their clasped hands, and smiled knowingly. She had already predicted something like this would happen, and had told Roger so the night before. "Congratulations! Looks like Christmas is certainly a magical holiday… with Ryan and Eva, and now you two… Oh, you all make me so happy." She grinned as she scooped another spoonful of the yogurt into her mouth.

"Thanks, Mom. Oh, are you still going into town today?"

"Why yes, I am!" Marina smiled. "Why do you ask?"

"I have to go away for a business thing with dad… It's just for today. Do you mind if Sarah accompanies you on your trip?" Hamilton explained as he sat down. Sarah mirrored his actions, sitting on his left.

"Of course! I'd be delighted if Sarah wanted to spend the day with little old me." Marina's eyes crinkled as she smiled with her eyes.

"Great." Hamilton grinned, before he checked his shiny silver watch. "Oops, I'm going to be late if I don't get on the road. I'll see you two later!" He planted a light kiss on Sarah's forehead. "Bye!"

"Have a safe trip, darling!" Marina called.

"I'll text you!" Sarah said.

And then there were two.

Marina turned towards Sarah with her lips curved, in a pretty smile. "I was thinking about leaving in around fifteen minutes. Is that okay with you?"

"That's perfectly fine." Sarah replied. "I'll go grab my bag, and meet you down here?"

"I look forward to it!" Marina said, finishing the last bits of her breakfast. She truly was looking forward to it. Sarah was a wonderful person, and now especially since she was involved with Hamilton, Marina wanted to get to know her better.

In fifteen minutes, Marina and Sarah were downstairs, in front of the large front door. They were ready to leave! Jerry had just handed Marina the keys and she was pulling on her coat when Sarah heard the tell-tale clacking that always preceded Eva's dramatic entrances. "Oh, hello, Eva!" Marina greeted her cheerfully.

"Hi, Mrs. Clouse! Are you two heading out?" Eva asked sweetly. Too sweetly, in Sarah's opinion. But she kept her mouth shut about that. Eva brushed a stray lock of her hair behind her ear, and the sparkling diamond on her left hand almost blinded Sarah. An amused look came over her face as she thought about how many times Eva would be doing that or something similar to show off her ring before the day ended.

"Yes, we are," Sarah said.

"That sounds fun!" Eva replied. "I'm not doing anything now too..." She was obviously fishing for an invite, and Sarah knew it would be rude not to invite her now after such an obvious hint, even though she wanted to spend some one-on-one time with Marina.

"Would you like to come?" Marina said kindly.

"I would be delighted to! Just let me grab my purse and I'll be right back!" Eva clacked away, leaving a powerful scent of J'adore behind.

***

An hour and ten minutes later, they were in town. Sarah had forgotten all about Eva and her annoying demeanor, because she was in complete awe of the town. Green and red sparkling lights hung on trees, and holiday music blared over speakers tied to lampposts. It cast a cheery holiday atmosphere over everything, and Sarah really loved it. Marina seemed to love it too, as she drove slowly in order to let Sarah and herself look at everything.

"Drive faster… by the time we get there, mall is going to close…" Sarah overheard Eva mutter under her breath in a very annoyed tone. Sarah raised an eyebrow, but didn't do anything about it.

"Are you enjoying the scenery, Eva?" Marina asked.

"Oh, yes, definitely! It's so pretty!" Eva said almost immediately.

Wow, Sarah thought. *That was so fake.* She had been suspicious about Eva's overly friendly personality earlier, and now her suspicions grew even deeper. Eva simply ignored Sarah for most of the car ride.

They reached the mall, and as soon as they stepped inside the warm building, Eva expressed her intention to go to every clothing store. How typical. Sarah and Marina trailed behind Eva as they went to store after store, eventually reaching Gucci, the store that Eva said she usually stayed the longest in. Marina spotted a watch store across the hall, and she made a mental note to go look at it after. Watches were perfect gifts for powerful men like her husband and sons.

"Ooh, I like this… and this… Oh, definitely this!" Eva muttered as she picked up shirt after shirt for herself, draping them over her thin arm. "Alright, off to the next section!" she exclaimed after she had accumulated a hefty amount of clothes from the contemporary section of the shop. Sarah wondered if by the end of the day, she'd need a truck to take all the clothes home.

Before Eva headed off, Marina stopped her. "I'll be going to the watch store just across the corridor, okay? I don't really need clothing at the moment, and I was thinking about purchasing a watch for Hamilton."

Sarah saw this as her chance to escape from Eva's shopping clutches. "Um… I'll come too!" she piped up and Marina grinned as they walked away from Eva, who acknowledged them with a nod before heading off to the next section.

As they walked out, Sarah spotted a sparkly black dress that she had not seen on the way in. It captured her attention, and when she felt the shimmery material in her hands, she fell in love with it even more. "Oh, that's gorgeous, Sarah!" Marina exclaimed. "I bet it would look great on you."

Sarah laughed humbly. "Oh, you really think so? Maybe I should go try it on…"

"Yes, go! I will wait for you," Marina offered.

"No, no, I can go by myself," Sarah said, not wanting to impose on Marina. "I'll join you in the watch shop after. I won't be long!" she promised.

"Alright, dear. I'll see you soon then!" Marina clutched her bag and exited the shop.

Sarah walked to look for the changing room, holding the slinky dress. She didn't go shopping that often, and it was rare that she found something that she really liked. After a minute or so, she found the changing rooms at the back of the store. Since this was a higher-end store, each changing room was rather large, and had plush chairs and several hooks that she assumed were to accommodate the absurd amount of clothes she was supposed to have, like Eva.

For some reason, the changing room attendant wasn't here like usual. The attendant had probably been called away by a customer for help. So after spending a couple minutes looking for an attendant, Sarah gave up. She just found a room on her own. There was only one other person in the changing room, and most of the rooms were free.

She stepped into a room and closed the door behind her quietly. She was just about to slip off her top when, all of a sudden, music started playing. It was some rendition of *My Milkshake,* and Sarah wondered who could have such an odd ringtone in such a classy shop.

"Hello?" A familiar voice answered the phone after a couple bars of music. Sarah recognized it as Eva. She must have decided to go to the changing room instead of the other section of the shop like she had planned. "Oh, hey, Teddy, baby! I missed you, sweetie."

"Baby? Sweetie?!" Sarah muttered under her breath. The term of endearment could have meant trouble, or it could have been harmless. Sarah had no idea which one it was.

"You'll never guess what Ryan did last night." There was a pause, as "Teddy," whoever he was, spoke. "Oh, don't worry, I checked earlier. There's no one around. If there were, I would have heard the changing room assistant get them a room, of course! Anyways, he finally proposed. It took so long for him to pick up the hints I was dropping, and I dropped a lot!"

Sarah was definitely surprised. Her mouth was open wide, and her brow was furrowed. This had the potential to go somewhere horrible, and fast. Ryan looked so happy with Eva, and Sarah had a dreadful feeling in the pit of her stomach that Eva was about to reveal that she didn't feel the same.

Eva trilled in laughter. "Yep, I'm so close to getting the family fortune. Well, yeah, I know Ryan's going to get boring after a while, but that's what affairs are for, silly! Mhm, the good girl act is really winning me points with the rest of the family, even though they're so *boring*. All of my efforts are coming to an end soon, and I'll be set for life! Then I can get you that new car, baby!" Eva giggled girlishly.

"No... I love *you* more!" Sarah rolled her eyes, thinking that Eva was so stereotypical. "Okay, I got to finish trying on these clothes. I'll talk to you later, darling!" She made two kissing noises before hanging up.

Sarah's heart was pounding. Eva was a terrible person! Should she tell Ryan? Was it her place to ruin a relationship? All these questions spun through her mind as she forgot about trying on the dress. She leaned against the door, contemplating her next action, when the door flew open suddenly, probably due to a faulty lock.

"Ah!" Sarah exclaimed, falling to the ground.

The sound was loud, and definitely alerted Eva that there was another presence in the changing rooms. Eva opened the door and her eyes widened as they happened upon Sarah, who was in the process of getting up. "How long have you been there?" Eva snarled viciously.

"I just got here seconds ago. I tripped." She was nervous, and when she was nervous, she had a tendency to start babbling. "The attendant wasn't here so I just came in myse—"

Sarah was rudely interrupted. "Did you hear anything?!" Eva questioned accusingly.

"No?" Sarah said, hoping it didn't come out like she was lying.

Eva seemed satisfied, but Sarah knew better than to think she was safe. "Fine." With a huff, Eva scowled before closing the door to the changing room again. Sarah regained composure, and returned into the changing room to try the dress on, all the while thinking about what Eva had said.

The rest of the shopping trip passed smoothly without further incident. They went for lunch afterwards at a charming restaurant that Marina picked. Sarah tried to be as friendly as possible, but it was hard because the conversation she had overheard with Eva still burned on her mind. Marina didn't seem to suspect anything. Eva, however, sent Sarah one chilling glare that made Sarah think that she was up to something. After a visit to a special Festival of Lights event in a nearby park and then dinner, Marina decided it was a good time to head back.

By the time the trio had returned to the house, it was already after nine. Sarah sighed as she headed up the stairs to her room, wondering what she was going to do. She had only been here for a couple days, but she had already discovered such a big secret. Would anyone even believe her if she revealed what she knew? After all, they had known Eva for a much longer time than her, and Eva knew how to charm people.

Just as she wondered if Hamilton was back, a polite knock came at her door.

"Come in." Her heart leaped as she hoped it was Hamilton.

It was.

"Hey, sweetie." He grinned, kissing her lightly on the lips. "I missed you."

"I missed you too," she murmured. "Did you fix the business thing?"

"That I did. Some lower-level associate was leaking info to a rival business." Hamilton sighed. "I hate people who do betray others for personal gain. But it's all settled now."

However happy she was to see him, he reminded her of his brother, which in turn made her think of Eva. Her brow furrowed slightly as she tried to expel those thoughts from her mind.

"Something wrong?" he asked, lightly planting kisses along her neck. He was intuitive.

"Mmm…" She debated telling him, but ultimately decided against it.

"Want to talk about it?"

She shook her head.

"Well, at least let me distract you," he whispered against her skin as he moved up towards her mouth, capturing it with his. He kissed her deeply and fiercely, one of his hands stroking her hair affectionately. His tongue slipped within her parted lips as their breaths mixed. They both knew where this was leading, and neither of them wanted it to stop.

They hungered for each other, and before long their clothes were off their bodies and cast onto the floor messily. They couldn't keep their hands off, and Hamilton wanted to explore every inch of her. This was the woman he was in love with, and he wanted to know everything about her. As their bodies entwined, there was a special connection between them that Hamilton could only describe as love.

For the first time, Hamilton made passionate love to her that night. And as his hands traveled across her skin, Sarah truly did feel her worries slip from her mind into oblivion.

Chapter 5

Sarah woke up in the morning completely naked, and very satisfied from the night's events. She was excited to spend Christmas Day with Hamilton today.

The previous night had been absolutely mind-blowing, and they both had cuddled sweetly before falling asleep. She stretched her arm out beside her but her hands were only met with the soft blanket and bedsheets. "Hmm…" Her hand hit upon a small piece of paper, which she picked up and read. *Hey, sweetie, I've just gone out for a walk with my father. I'll see you at breakfast. Hope you slept well. Yours, Hamilton.* Hamilton had scrawled a sweet message onto it with his gorgeous cursive handwriting. Sarah smiled dreamily as she held the paper close to her chest.

Sarah turned to her other side and grabbed her phone while gently dropping the slip of paper on the nightstand. There were texts waiting for her, from Terrence, asking if she had gotten the first draft of the article finished yet, and instructing her to call him as soon as she woke, even if it were still early.

Hamilton's words from last night suddenly echoed in her mind. *I hate people who do betray others for personal gain.*

How would he react when the article came out with all these personal facts and photos about his family and home? Her name would be attached to the article too. He would think that she didn't really love him... Sarah's heart raced. Was there any chance she could convince Terrence to not run the article?

She pressed the call button, it rang once before Terrence picked it up. "Sarah! Have you finished the first draft? Have you sent it to me? I've been expecting it! Don't make me act like a teenage girl and refresh my mailbox every five minutes!"

"No... And Terrence... Is there any chance we don't have to run the article...?" she asked hesitantly.

"Of course not! Stop joking, Sarah. You know how important this piece is to Rumor." He laughed. "Don't you still want that promotion?"

Sarah thought about Marina's friendly face, Roger's welcoming personality and Hamilton's loving embrace. Her mind then flickered to how disappointed and heartbroken Hamilton would be if he found out. That image made her feel unfathomably sad. She couldn't betray him. Sure, Pulse was important, but she could always get another job with another magazine... right?

"I can't write the article, Terrence," she whimpered.

Terrence's tone changed almost immediately. "Excuse me? Sarah, as an employee, you will write and report what you are told!" he roared.

"I really can't, Terrence, please forgive me."

"Have you forgotten all I've done for you? Sarah!" He was yelling now. "Sarah, don't you dare screw me over on this!"

"I have no choice…"

"Why can't you write the article?" he asked, lowering his voice, but the anger still seeped through. "Explain your reasons."

"I… I just don't think it'd be fair to the Clouses."

"They're used to being in the paper. What's another article or two? Come on, Sarah, you have an inside scoop! These are about as rare as shooting stars."

Sarah bit her lip, mulling it over, but returning back to her previous decision. "I'm sorry, Terrence, I can't. I really can't."

"Sarah, I'm going to ask you one last time. Are you sure?" She could hear the disappointment in his voice.

"I'm sure."

"Alright then. I have no choice… but to let you go. Come gather your things as soon as you can. I cannot have a journalist on my team that requires such goading and cannot follow orders on such an important article." He sounded cold now, detached.

"I'm sorry, Terrence." Three quiet beeps signalled the end of the call.

Sarah sat on her bed and sighed. She just lost her job, but she still felt like she had done the right thing. She had confidence she would be able to find another magazine that was willing to hire her. All that mattered now was that it was all over.

It was still early in the morning, and Sarah flung herself onto her bed. There was still some time before breakfast, and Sarah wanted to forget about the whole thing. Quickly, she fell into a deep, dreamless sleep.

An hour or so later, Sarah awoke to the sound of loud, impatient knocking on the door, which was unusual for Hamilton. "Who is it?" Sarah called as she pulled on a shirt and sat up.

"It's me," Eva's voice trilled, very loudly. Without an invitation, she opened the door and her eyes narrowed upon seeing Sarah on the bed. In her tight sweater and leggings, she looked very fashionable. It made Sarah feel a little awkward, as she was only wearing a shirt. Eva closed the door behind her, and there was a wicked smile playing on her face.

Uh-oh, Sarah thought. That look couldn't mean anything good.

"What do you want, Eva?"

"I'm going to cut the bull and get straight to the point. I had a bad feeling about you from the first time I met you. So I did a little research. And imagine my surprise when I find that you work for a tabloid magazine!" Eva smirked as she lifted a hand to her face in a mock thinking pose. "Shall I tell the family?"

Eva reveled in Sarah's shocked expression.

"Please don't." Sarah didn't want to beg, but if push came to shove, she would do it. It wasn't like Sarah now worked for Rumor, but she knew that it would just seem like excuses she made up if she told them she had been fired. It would break Hamilton's heart.

"I won't, on one condition. You leave. Before the end of the day. Take your car, and just go. Don't tell anyone that you're leaving. Especially not Hamilton," Eva said bitterly.

"Do you really have to do this? Eva... I love him." Sarah had a feeling that no matter what she said, at this point, Eva would not change her mind. "Please, reconsider."

"Yeah, right." Eva rolled her eyes. "Nothing's gonna make me let you out of this."

Sarah sighed, knowing that Eva would stay true to her words. She had no doubt about that. Though she still did not understand why Eva wanted to hurt her so, there was now no use to think about reasons. Seeing no way out, Sarah agreed. "Fine. You win,

Eva," she said with resignation. "Why do you even hate me so much?" She blinked back tears, not wanting to give Eva the satisfaction of seeing her cry. She was thinking about how to tell Hamilton that she was leaving.

Eva didn't even give her an answer. "Marina told me to call you down for breakfast." She brushed the earlier question aside easily. With a sassy flip of her long hair, Eva stalked away with a new spring in her step. "Merry Christmas!"

Sarah sighed as she dressed completely and walked downstairs, her heart heavy. She would probably leave after breakfast. She wanted to see Hamilton one last time. Leaving on her own would be the best way out. If Hamilton knew about Rumor, he would be completely devastated and she would end up having to leave anyway.

She was unusually quiet during the first half an hour, focusing solely on eating and not making much conversation. Hamilton wrapped an arm around her, and it only made her feel worse. Eva was animated, very happy that her plan to get rid of Sarah had succeeded.

All of a sudden, Ryan's phone beeped. It was a different ring tone than his usual one, and it immediately put him on high alert. "Ryan! No phones at the table!" Marina exclaimed. "You know the rules."

"Mom, this is a special ring tone. I set it to get alerts if anything about us gets into those tabloid magazines so we can deal with it quickly if it's fake or really bad for our reputation. Hamilton suggested I set it up!" Ryan grinned at his big brother before checking his phone. Slowly, his face fell as he read. "How…"

"What's wrong, honey?" Marina watched the confusion appear on Ryan's face.

"This magazine. They posted about the proposal. Even about the inside details. The style of the ring. How I did it. Who it's to. How did they get this information!? Hell, there's even information about our house and dad's collections!" Ryan exclaimed angrily.

"Which magazine is it?" Eva asked innocently. Sarah had a terrible sense that something bad was about to happen.

"Um… Rumor."

Sarah's eyes widened in surprise. She had only told Terrence about the actual proposal itself, but had said nothing about the ring and other details! How had he gotten the information? It certainly wasn't her. Then she realized this was the perfect moment for Eva to rat her out, to destroy her in the eyes of the Clouses forever.

But she wouldn't do that, would she?

They had a deal! She was already prepared to leave. She looked at Eva with her owl-like eyes. She was begging her not to say anything on the inside.

Eva returned her glare, and a smile played on her lips as she mulled over the choices in her mind. She enjoyed the way it made Sarah squirm. *This is torture,* Sarah thought, grimacing.

Eva leaned forwards, placed one well-manicured hand on her made-up cheek before she spoke. "I think I know who did it."

Sarah's heart fell into her stomach. She knew what was going to happen next. Though she was sitting, her legs began to shake. Her face turned ashen. It must have been because she had overheard that conversation in the changing room. It must be because Eva wanted to discredit everything Sarah said, just in case Sarah had heard her plans.

Eva's eyes were locked onto hers, and slowly everyone turned to stare at Sarah too, following Eva's gaze.

"What…?" Hamilton said so quietly it almost sounded like a whisper. "Sarah?" He looked at her, hoping, praying that Eva was wrong.

All the blood drained from Sarah's face, turning it even whiter than before. "Um…" she stammered. She could barely form coherent thoughts, and she was painfully aware that it made her look very, very guilty.

"Really?" Ryan interrupted the tense moment. "Is it really Sarah?"

Eva nodded, and suddenly turned from the bad girl into a sweet angel. "I... I didn't want to tell everyone this. I honestly did not want this to happen. But I recognized her when I was reading one of the magazines and her name was in the article... When I asked Sarah about it to confirm... she threatened me not to tell."

Eva paused and Sarah scowled on the inside. Eva was quite the actress.

"But... I don't want to keep secrets from everyone. She... She's a journalist for Rumor magazine!" Eva exclaimed finally, as a hush fell over the table.

Hamilton cleared his throat. "Sarah... Is this true?" Pain was reflected in his eyes. He wanted to give her the benefit of the doubt. He longed for her to tell him that this was all just some sort of misunderstanding.

Eva didn't even give Sarah a chance to respond. "If you look in her room... She has a camera. She took pictures of us. On her phone too. I saw her do it during the proposal."

"Can we see your phone, Sarah?" Marina asked gently.

Sarah knew that if she protested, it would only be worse, and they'd end up seeing it anyway. So, voluntarily, she unlocked it and handed it over.

Marina gasped slightly as she saw the pictures of the proposal. Disappointment reflected in her eyes, something that Sarah hated. She would much rather Marina get mad at her, yell at her, call her names. But instead, one by one, the Clouses all looked at her with quiet disappointment.

A single tear escaped Sarah's eye. "It wasn't me. It really wasn't me who leaked it!" she protested, but by the looks on their faces, they had already made up their minds.

Hamilton was staring at her with mixed emotions. "Is that why you…" He pressed fingers to his lips, then quickly lowered them again. But Sarah knew what he had meant.

"No, Hamilton, no! My feelings for you are real!" she pleaded, not caring that his entire family was sitting there and that she was probably making a fool of herself. Her head was spinning, and she could barely think straight. How could it have all gone downhill so fast?

His eyes, previously so sad and emotional, changed. They became indifferent. Sarah realized that he probably would no longer listen to her. He probably saw her now as some cruel, conniving journalist who was willing to do anything for her next scoop. Though it was true that she had started off that way, she had now fallen in love with him, and had given up even her job for him. But now it was all useless.

"I think... I think you'd better leave, Sarah." Hamilton's voice was eerily calm as he spoke. His hands were balled into fists, and she could see that it was taking him a lot of strength and self-control to stay so impassive. "And... I think it would be best if we don't see each other again."

"It's not me..." Sarah felt like a broken record as she whimpered out the phrase one last time. But resigned to her fate, Sarah pushed back her chair. The scraping of wood upon wood was loud against the silence.

"Goodbye," Sarah said with an air of finality.

As she walked out, she looked back and stole one last glance at Hamilton, hoping that he was watching her. But her heart fell when she realized that no one was paying any attention to her. They were completely done with her, weren't they?

She walked upstairs, feeling a sort of numbness in her body. So this was how it was all going to end. She knew it was too good to be true. The rich, handsome, successful business executive falling for her? She should have known better.

She shouldn't have let herself fall in love with him.

But she did, and now that was her cross to bear.

As she hadn't brought much, the packing only took around ten minutes. Before long, she was ready to leave, even though her heart was begging her to stay. As she headed down the stairs for the very last time, she spotted Jerry at the front door. "Hi, Jerry," she greeted him.

Jerry nodded formally as he handed her the keys to her car, as if she were a stranger. "Goodbye, Ms. Armstrong." Of course, Jerry had already heard of the incident, which was probably why he was behaving so icily towards her.

With a sigh, Sarah took the keys from him. "Bye. Um, thanks for everything," she murmured as she headed out into the cold winter air.

She looked back at the house before getting into her car. She could see the window of the dining room, and the curtains were drawn. The family were probably comforting Hamilton inside, and Eva was probably making up some more lies to further convince the family of how evil Sarah was and how they were all much better off without her.

Sarah's hands shook as she pulled out of the driveway and drove down the long road. She was struggling not to become emotional, and she just wanted to go home as fast as possible so she could bury herself in a book and a glass of wine in bed.

She passed the crossroads where she and Hamilton had first met, and it brought a fresh set of tears to her eyes. They clouded her vision and she realized that she couldn't drive anymore. So she pulled over onto the side of the road, and pressed her hands over her face. Her breaths were shallow, and she tried to calm herself down.

"Come on, Sarah. Breathe," she instructed herself. "Get it together. After all, you've only known him for a couple of days. It's crazy for you to feel so heartbroken about it." But even as she said these words, she knew they weren't true. Hamilton meant more to her than a holiday fling. She had fallen for him, and fallen hard.

Sarah felt like an idiot, but she couldn't lie to herself. Her chest felt so hollow, like someone had reached in and ripped out her heart. Her mind kept traveling back to Hamilton, how he had looked the last time she saw him. The pain in his eyes had been too much.

Wiping her tears away with the back of her hand, Sarah knew that she couldn't sit on the side of the road and mope about it for hours. It was pathetic. So she switched on the radio to a rock station, the kind of music that always helped her forget her troubles. Turning the volume up, Sarah drove towards the city, towards home, doing her very best to push Hamilton and the Clouses out of her mind.

Chapter 6

Unfortunately, though she wanted to default to her usual distraction of work, she now was out of work to throw herself into. It was soon incredibly clear that she needed to find another magazine to write for, and soon!

She had some money saved up that she could use for bills, but after almost two full weeks of unemployment, Sarah began to worry about her future. She also had way too much time on her hands, and that allowed her to think about Hamilton, which was the exact opposite of what she wanted. Sarah missed him more than she could soberly admit to herself. Of course, she had experienced breakups before, with relationships much longer than this one, but they had never hurt this much. She hadn't known anything could hurt this much.

Sarah groaned as she buried her face in her pillow. How was she ever going to forget about him? She knew she sounded like a love-struck teenager. For an adult, she knew that she really should know better. Yet she still felt like something was missing in her life, and it hurt to know that she could never get that something back. It felt like the end of the world, though she hated being melodramatic.

She had given Hamilton her address, and she wondered if he still kept it saved in his phone as he had entered the address into it that one night, and had promised that he would never lose it. He had probably deleted her number, the address, and the pictures they had taken together. She had thought that once she returned to her daily life, everything would be perfect. But now, it seemed like it was the exact opposite of that.

Suddenly, interrupting her depressing thoughts, her computer began to jingle. She was getting a video call from Victoria! It was perfect, just what she needed to cheer herself up. "Hey, Vic." Sarah put on the best neutral face she could as she answered the call.

Victoria frowned almost immediately. "Hey, girl, something wrong?" Sarah had always praised Victoria for her incredible intuition, but now she cursed it. She knew talking about Hamilton would probably make her emotional again, something she wanted to avoid.

"Do you know Hamilton Clouse?" Sarah asked. Victoria nodded, and Sarah continued speaking. "I had to scope out his place for an article and we… kind of ended up falling in love. But Hamilton found out that I worked for Rumor, which made his entire family think that I was only with them because of the article." She gave Victoria the summarized version of the story. She could always tell the full one later.

"Oh, damn. S, I'm so sorry that had to happen. I wish I could come give you a hug but I'm halfway across the world." Victoria's lips pursed. "Wait, worked? Past tense?"

"Yeah… Well I sort of refused to publish the article for Terrence because I was in love with Hamilton and I didn't want him to think I was there solely for information… But I guess it was all in vain because it happened anyway." Sarah sighed, "I guess it's like the old saying, fortune doesn't favor fools."

"Aw, S…" Victoria sighed, wishing she could be there for her best friend. Sarah was never the type to fall in love easily, so she knew that this was serious.

"Yeah… I know it's pretty dumb to fall in love in only a couple days. I don't know if it was the holiday atmosphere or maybe I was just feeling lonely but… It felt so real." Sarah couldn't help but smile wistfully as she easily recalled Hamilton's kind eyes, his gentle and sweet words. But those eyes swiftly turned into ones that reflected hurt and those were the ones that remained in her mind. "But now, I just can't get that look of betrayal he had on his face out of my mind."

Victoria allowed a sad smile to appear on her face. It had been too long since she had seen her best friend in love, even if now it were a sad kind of love. "I don't think it's dumb at all. Actually, it's kind of beautiful. And honestly… honey, you know I'm a firm believer in love. And I don't think Hamilton would have been so upset if he weren't truly in love with you."

"I guess that's true."

"Trust me, Sarah, if it's meant to be, it'll find a way to work itself out. And hell, even if it doesn't, I'll personally hook you up with some of my friends." Victoria winked playfully.

"Oh, God, no, Vic, I remember the last 'friend' you set me up with." Sarah used her fingers to make sarcastic air quotes. "I also remember his crazy, heavy flirting and trying to get into my pants within the first ten minutes of the date! Also, he wouldn't stop talking about different kinds of cheese and hockey!"

"Okay, fine, that date, I'll admit, was a bit of a wreck. Hey, in my defense, he's totally normal to me." Victoria laughed, and Sarah joined her.

For the next little while, there was nothing but the sounds of their joking and laughter. It completely distracted Sarah, and she really appreciated it. But Victoria couldn't stay with her online forever, and when Victoria left, Sarah was left alone once again with her thoughts.

But Victoria had given Sarah some new hope for the future. Maybe it all would work out. And hopefully for the better.

***

As Sarah tried to put Hamilton from her mind, Hamilton was trying to do the same for her. He just kept thinking about how Sarah had looked after he had told her to never call again. It was hard for him to believe that she had really gotten so close to him just to get information for her next article.

At least she hadn't cried. Crying was his absolute weakness. He knew that if she had allowed a single tear to escape her warm eyes, he would have broken down and ran to take her into his arms. He probably would have forgiven her, just for a little while.

God, he loved her. But no matter how much he missed her, he still couldn't forgive her. Even though it had seemed so unlikely for her to be an undercover journalist, a quick Google search had revealed that Sarah did indeed write several articles for Rumor, and she had been rather secretive about her job. The camera and those photos in her phone were such damning evidence too. And even if he wanted to give her the benefit of the doubt, it was much too hard to.

Even when he was at work, he found his mind drifting back to Sarah. Usually, his work was the perfect distraction but it had been a somewhat lax week, and that allowed him way too much time to think.

The way her pretty face lit up when she smiled at him and the way she called his name haunted him. He very rarely turned to drink for temporary relief, but he was now close to that.

After two weeks of this torture, Hamilton realized that he needed some help. He needed someone to talk to, someone who wouldn't judge him too harshly. So he hopped into his car and drove towards his parents' penthouse after giving his mother a call to let her know that he was on his way.

Marina opened the door with a warm smile. She had been expecting him, ever since the holiday incident. They had all refrained from talking about Sarah after she had left. They didn't want to upset him further. Eva hadn't really followed that silent rule and had played the role of the victim, finally "free" from Sarah's "bullying." Marina hadn't pegged Sarah to be a manipulative reporter, but some people were just good at lying.

"Hi, honey, come in." She gave her eldest son a warm hug.

"Hi, Mom," he said. He rarely called her that anymore, usually preferring the formal "mother" ever since he had matured when he went to college. But now, he felt like a kid again, in need of his mom's embrace and reassurance.

"Now, I'm pretty sure I know why you're here. Is it about Sarah?" Hamilton followed Marina into the living room, where piping hot mugs of cocoa were waiting for them. A maid was setting down a plate of cookies. She nodded her head politely when she spotted Hamilton, and shot him a warm smile.

"Hi, Mina." He waited until Mina left the room before sitting down. "Yeah… Mom, you're right, it is about Sarah," Hamilton admitted. "I can't stop thinking about her."

Marina sat beside her son, who was so tall and big, but now needed his mother's help. It was a little adorable. "Hmm…" Marina hummed as she thought. "Oh, son, you're really in love with her. I can see it on your face."

"It's never been like this before. Not even with Leah." Hamilton groaned. Leah was the girl he had proposed to years before, but she had turned him down. It had hurt so incredibly, but eventually he did realize that they were never meant to be together. This longing that he had now was on par, perhaps even more than it had been all those years ago.

"Oh, Hamilton…" Marina patted him on the back affectionately. "I know you love her so much, but you can't forgive her for the magazine business, right? And I don't blame you. It is a terrible thing to do. But somehow, I can't really imagine her doing it." Marina had genuinely liked Sarah, and believed Sarah to be a kind girl, but she had to concede that the evidence against her was irrefutable.

"I know, Mom. It's just so unbelievable, yet all the evidence is there, staring me in the face. And the only reasonable conclusion is that she really was with me to get information. Otherwise, why would she have been driving on the road towards our place when I crashed into her? She told me she doesn't have any family that she was visiting up here too... And she was being secretive about her job the entire time that she stayed with us." Hamilton sighed. "Plus Eva even said Sarah threatened her."

"Really... That Eva likes to make things up for dramatic effect. I won't deny that Sarah took the photos, but I do have to say that I doubt she threatened Eva." Marina was always excellent at reading people, and she was rarely wrong. To her, Sarah had appeared genuine in her personality, the way she spoke, and the kind way she behaved. But Hamilton had raised an irrefutable point about the photographic evidence.

"What should I do?" He asked Marina the same question that men had been asking their mothers for generations. "I can't focus on anything other than her. I even yelled at an intern today when he didn't deserve it at all."

"If you ask me... I think Sarah deserves the benefit of the doubt. Maybe you should go straight to the source, and talk to her boss or the owner of the magazine. Maybe he can tell you who really gave him the information. And if it really is Sarah, then at least you'll know for sure." Marina suggested an idea that made Hamilton smile.

He reached over and hugged his mom tightly. "That's actually an amazing idea, Mom."

"That's what I'm here for!" Marina chirped happily, glad she had been able to be helpful. "I know you won't rest until you find out the truth." It had been a trait he had brought with him from his childhood, and she found it rather endearing.

"You always have the best ideas." Hamilton grinned. "I love you, Mom."

"I love you too, darling. Now go. You don't want to miss your chance," she urged. It was a quick visit and she had wanted Hamilton to stay longer, but there was only half an hour to 5 p.m. when most businesses closed, and Marina wanted her son to go and find out what really happened. "Good luck, honey."

"Thanks, Mom." He gave her one last hug before walking out of the house and towards his car. Sitting in the front seat, he pulled out his phone and did a quick Google search. It didn't take him long to find the headquarters of the place, right in the city.

Hamilton was never good with directions, but at least he had the helpful GPS to guide him along. He drove as fast as he could towards the heart of the city, where he knew he would finally be able to find out what happened, once and for all.

He was strangely nervous, and found that his hands shook slightly. His heart pounded as he wondered what kind of person Sarah's boss would be. Would he tell Hamilton that Sarah was a terrible employee? That she was always late, bullied other coworkers, and was just generally a miserable person? Or would he tell Hamilton that she was such a wonderful girl, and she was the one that had boosted their magazine's sales with the information?

The possibilities were endless in his mind, and he knew that overthinking it wouldn't help at all. But it was hard to stop. There were too many variables. If Sarah had been telling the truth, if she really wasn't the one that had leaked the information, then who did? Roger? Ryan?

Hamilton breathed out a heavy sigh. Whatever the answer, he would be finding out very, very soon. There were an unusually large amount of cars crowded on the road, and a traffic jam was in place. "Damn it," he swore as the other drivers' tempers began to flare.

"Hey, blockhead, move it!" A driver leaned out of his open car window and shook his fist angrily at the woman in front of him, who shot him the middle finger back.

Hamilton looked at his watch. Was he going to make it in time?

By the time Hamilton reached the tall office building, it was five minutes after five. *I hope her boss hasn't left yet. Whoever this Terrence Evans was, he better not have left already.* Hamilton scanned the listing of office floors before stepping into an elevator.

It rose too slowly, and he was starting to feel impatient. He needed to know the truth behind the story leak. When the doors finally slid open after what felt like an eternity, he realized that his palms were sweaty. His breathing was short and choppy, and his heart raced. He hadn't even thought about what he was going to say to Terrence if he did catch him.

Hamilton rushed to the front desk, but was dismayed to find that the secretary had already left. He groaned, frustrated, before he dashed further into the floor. He passed cubicle after cubicle, his eyes scanning for Terrence's office. At the very corner of the floor, a glass office stood. The name plate neatly read Terrence Evans. But alas, it was empty. Hamilton sighed. Of course, he would have left already. God forbid he have any bit of luck.

In fact, a quick scan around the office floor showed that there was only one person left at her cubicle, headphones in, and basically zoning out from her surroundings. The woman looked up at Hamilton, and removed an earbud. "Can I help y—?" Then she realized who he was. "Hamilton Clouse?" she said incredulously.

"Yes, that's me," he said.

The woman realized that he was even better looking in person than he was in the papers, and she almost immediately straightened her hair and sucked in her stomach. She knew he was single, and was a very eligible bachelor. "Hi, I'm Amy," she said with a huge grin. "How can I help you?"

"I'm looking for Terrence Evans. Is he still here?" he said curtly, not really paying attention to her attempts to make herself look better.

"I don't think so. But let me check in the employee room. You can wait here." Amy flashed him another brilliant smile.

"Thanks."

Amy deliberately walked slowly, her pert behind swaying from side to side deliberately as she hoped Hamilton was watching her. He wasn't.

A man followed Amy out of the employee room in the back. He had his coat on, and a bag by his side. He also looked very irritated. "Really, Amy, I'm just about to leave. I have a dinner planned with my wife."

"You're not going to want to miss this!" she persuaded, pulling him towards Hamilton.

"Who's that?" Terrence didn't recognize him at first either, and just thought he was another stranger or someone here to protest about something they had printed in the magazine. "Who are you?" he demanded.

"Hamilton. Hamilton Clouse," Hamilton answered, and waited for the flash of recognition to hit.

"Ah! Mr. Clouse... Might I ask, what are you doing here?" Terrence walked over and shook Hamilton's hand.

"I need some information."

"Come into my office." Terrence already had a feeling that he knew what this was going to be about.

Amy harrumphed, knowing that she wasn't invited to this meeting. She wanted to talk to Hamilton a bit more, to try and get him interested in her, but it looked like she wasn't going to be getting that chance. She returned to her seat and popped her earbuds back in as Hamilton and Terrence walked into his office.

"How can I help you, Mr. Clouse?" Terrence sat back in his chair, and set his bag down.

"As I said earlier, I need some information. A certain journalist by the name of Sarah works here, correct?" Hamilton started formally, entwining his hands within themselves as he sat back in his chair.

"Why do you want to know?" Terrence's eyes narrowed in suspicion. Had something big happened during Sarah's trip to Hamilton's home? Is that why she had refused to publish the article and why he was now here, questioning her whereabouts? Terrence knew better than to outright give information. After all, information was a journalist's life, and could not be taken lightly.

Hamilton had been expecting some resistance. After all, a man at Terrence's level would not have been able to get there without expert negotiation skills. "Personal reasons," he replied very generally.

"Well, I can tell you that Sarah was a journalist here, yes. But that's all."

"Was?" Hamilton's eyebrow raised curiously. "Why the past tense?"

"She is no longer employed here," Terrence said without any sympathy.

"And why is that?"

"Not so fast. If you want me to tell you that… You'll have to give me a reason to." The implication was clear in his statement.

Hamilton sighed. "What do you want to know?"

"Well… I know that you Clouses like staying away from the spotlight… With the exception of Ryan, of course. Having an inside scoop into the lavish life of you and your family right from the horse's mouth would certainly be helpful to our magazine's reputation."

Hamilton knew that he didn't want to be in the papers, like his mother and father, but he wanted this information so badly. He had a pressing feeling that Sarah was innocent, and had not intended on falling in love with him only to get information. He didn't know what he was going to do if Terrence revealed detrimental information, but no matter what, he just had to know.

"Fine. I'll agree to an interview," Hamilton grumbled. "And I will answer the questions to the best of my ability."

Terrence grinned. An exclusive interview with Hamilton Clouse! That would certainly be reputation boosting. Hamilton rarely gave interviews, usually preferring to let his younger brother take the spotlight, but plenty of women found him attractive, and his mysterious nature only made him more interesting.

"It's a deal."

"Now, tell me why Sarah left the magazine."

"I fired her," Terrence said easily. "She disobeyed my orders regarding a very important article, so I had no choice but to let her go."

"I'm going to need more detail than that." Hamilton's heart started to beat a little quicker. Was she innocent? Was she really innocent?

"As you have probably seen, we recently published an article on your family. More specifically, Ryan's proposal to his now-fiancée, Eva." Terrence paused, and Hamilton nodded in response. "Sarah was fired because she refused to publish an article she had written about the proposal. I don't know why, but she simply said she wasn't going to. It would have been an incredibly big scoop, for the magazine and her journalistic career, and she almost ruined the former. I don't need irresponsible journalists like that on my team."

"I think I know why…" Hamilton murmured to himself, a ghost of a smile playing on his lips. It really wasn't Sarah! "So, who was the source then?" The smile disappeared, replaced with a slight frown. He had a nasty feeling about who it was, and if his hunch was true, Ryan would be heartbroken.

Terrence hesitated for a moment, but remembered how Hamilton's interview would greatly improve the magazine's popularity. "Eva." He watched Hamilton's face as he revealed this information. There was no surprise, no great gasp of realization. Hamilton had always known Eva was a rotten apple, but he had always hoped she had truly been in love with Ryan.

"Eva…" Hamilton echoed mournfully. He would have to be the one that broke it to Ryan and that weighed heavily on his heart. But it wasn't Sarah. Thank God, it wasn't Sarah.

"Yes, Eva has been our source for several stories now. She has always managed to get inside information, and has been helping us for quite a while now." Hamilton nodded, understanding that it was not Terrence's fault that Eva had decided to use her relationship in a less-than-ethical manner.

Hamilton stood up, and held out his hand towards Terrence. "Thank you for all your help, Terrence." He pulled his wallet out of his pocket, and pulled out a rectangular white card from it. "This is my card. Please call when you would like to set up the interview." It would be irritating to go through the whole interview process, but it was worth it, because now he knew that Sarah had played no part in the whole release.

"Ah, Mr. Clouse, I will have to ask that you refrain from revealing that our source is Ms. Eva publicly in any interviews, public forums or whatnot," Terrence added.

"That will be no problem at all," Hamilton agreed good-naturedly. "Have a good day." He knew that he certainly would. He just had one stop to make, before he would go to Sarah's place and win her back.

Chapter 7

After he had finished his business, he programmed the GPS for Sarah's address, which he had neatly saved in his phone when she had told him, so many days ago. Forgetting it was the last thing he had wanted to do.

The earlier wave of traffic had died down somewhat, but not as much as he would have liked. He sat in his toasty warm car, grateful that he had gotten around to getting the heater fixed. Soft droplets of snow were beginning to fall, and it made for a pretty scene, even though Hamilton was stuck in traffic.

It gave him time to think about what he was going to say to Sarah.

Was she even going to be home?

He really hoped she would be. He knew he had to apologize for the incredibly accusing and rude way he had acted towards her, but he had no idea if she would actually believe him and trust him again. After all, he hadn't believed her when she asked him to in the moment she needed him most.

Slowly, Hamilton made his way to the front of her apartment building. He was suddenly aware that his heart was pounding like a jackhammer. He took deep, cleansing breaths in an attempt to calm himself down. It worked, but just barely.

He rode the elevator anxiously, staring at the mirror lining the walls. He didn't look all that nervous, which was good. His chocolate hair looked impeccably gelled, and his suit, immaculately pressed, looked fantastic on him, like usual. Hamilton let out a long breath.

Damn it, he was Hamilton Clouse! And he was going to get the girl of his dreams back.

Ding! The elevator doors slid open, and Hamilton checked his phone for the fifth time since he had left the car, just to make sure he had the right door number in mind. Each step he took down the long, carpeted hallway seemed to increase the pounding in his head. He was torn between confidence and doubt.

Then, he was at her door. He stood in front of it, staring at the golden numbers stuck onto the wooden door, spelling out six-oh-nine. "Here we go," he murmured quietly before raising his hand and knocked onto the smooth surface.

There was no answer for the first minute, and a dreadful feeling was coming over him that she wasn't home. He knocked again, this time louder. This time, the lock turned and the door was pulled open. And there she was.

***

The last person Sarah was expecting to see when she opened her door was Hamilton. But nevertheless, there he was, standing in front of her in his handsome business suit. His hair looked gorgeous like usual, and his deep blue eyes were just as she had remembered them. God, she couldn't help but feel a flutter within her heart as she gazed at him. But seeing him also reminded her of all the pain he had caused.

"Sarah..." he started.

"What are you doing here, Hamilton?" she interrupted him. It still hurt, the way he had so harshly embarrassed her and cast her out of his home after not believing her. "I thought you never wanted to see me again."

"Sarah, please listen to me. I know you didn't leak the story. And I'm so sorry." He knew that at that point, if she had wanted him to beg for forgiveness, he would have done it. "Sarah... Let me come in and explain everything to you, please."

She mulled it over in her head. She wanted to let him in so badly, but a part of her still ached from the biting words he had thrown at her before. Could she trust him again? But even though her brain was telling her that it was a bad idea, her heart wrenched at the thought of letting him go.

"Fine. You get ten minutes," she said as she opened the door wider and he swept in. She breathed in his scent, and remembered the magical nights they had spent together during Christmas. It still made her heart ache. *Oh, you're so weak, Sarah,* she scolded herself in her thoughts. "Come to the living room."

Sarah, clad in a simple floral bathrobe, strode across the floor in her fuzzy slippers. A half-finished glass of wine and a novel, which he had interrupted her from, sat on the coffee table in front of a sofa. She sank down into an armchair, picked up the wine and stared at him with her big blue eyes.

Hamilton sat down on the loveseat adjacent to her, and he locked his orbs onto hers. He pressed his hands together, entwining them before beginning to twiddle his thumbs. He had gone over so many possible things to say in his head, but he had mysteriously forgotten everything. So he decided that perhaps the truth would be the best.

"Sarah, I know I hurt you. A lot. I can't even begin to express how sorry I am that I hurt you so much. I wish I could take back what I said, but I can't."

Sarah could feel the tears welling from the corners of her eyes, and took a sip of wine to distract herself. The alcohol buzzed through her body, helping, but only slightly.

His hands were shaking slightly, but he pressed on. "The absolute truth is, Sarah, that I love you. Even though we've only spent several days together, I've felt more of a connection with you than I have had with anyone before. You just seem to understand me, even when I don't understand myself. I should have believed you. I really should have, and I feel like such a failure that I hadn't. I went to your old office today. You never told me that you were fired because you wanted to protect my family and me. Eva was the one who had given all the information to the magazine. I'm so sorry I didn't trust you." Hamilton took a deep breath.

"Hamilton, I tried so hard to forget you after you said that you never wanted to see me again. And I... It was so unbelievably tough for me." She wasn't able to hold her tears back now, and one droplet of the clear liquid crept silently down her soft cheek. "And now you're telling me all these things... It's so overwhelming."

"I know it will be a challenge for you to trust me again, but I promise to do everything in my power to prove my worth to you." Hamilton reached into his jacket, and pulled out a small velvet box.

Sarah's eyes widened in surprise. "I-is that...?" Her heart was now beginning to pound. A ring box? He was going to propose? She definitely was *not* ready for that.

99

Hamilton read Sarah's face easily. "Ah, no, it's not a marriage proposal. But it is a ring." He opened the box slowly, and took Sarah's breath away. It was a beautiful silver ring, with a brilliantly blue, oval sapphire in the middle, surrounded by tiny diamonds. It was her birthstone, and her favorite color. "Sarah, I never want to lose you again. These two weeks have seemed like an eternity without you. With this promise ring, if you will accept it, I pledge to never leave you again. I promise to love you with all my heart, to the best of my ability. Please."

Sarah could barely breathe.

"Oh my… Hamilton… I…" Sarah stuttered out. She loved this man so much. How could she say no? But the hurt she had suffered at his hands still remained in the back of her mind.

His eyes were begging her to say yes.

"Hamilton… I accept," she finally said in a trembling voice.

He moved closer to her as a big smile bloomed onto his face. He plucked the ring from its white cushion and gently took her left hand. He slowly slid it onto her middle finger, smiling brightly at her when she lifted it up to the light to admire how it looked. He knew that it would look amazing on her.

"You look so beautiful," Hamilton said as he stood up and pulled her into his arms. "How could I have ever let you go?" he murmured as he leaned down and kissed her on her soft lips. At first she resisted, but slowly, she sank into his embrace.

Sarah wrapped her arms around him instinctively as he hugged her, feeling his warmth against her. "I love you," he whispered into her ear. "Truly."

She relaxed as she leaned into his kiss. She knew that this was where she belonged, and she finally felt that maybe, just maybe, everything was going to turn out alright after all.

Epilogue

"Sarah Armstrong, will you marry me?"

With that sentence, spoken during one romantic evening, half a year after Hamilton had given her the promise ring, it had all begun. Months of talking to caterers, finding locations, finding a pastor, making invitations, even sorting through a million different flower arrangements, were all building towards this one day. And everyone was definitely elated.

Sarah stood in her gorgeous white gown, staring at the mirror in front of her. This dress was designed just for her, and Marina had insisted on buying it for Sarah as a wedding present. After Sarah and Hamilton, Marina was the one that was looking forward the most to this wedding. After all, her baby son was going to be married!

Marina clasped her hands happily together as she gazed at the beautiful figure of her soon-to-be daughter-in-law. "Oh, Sarah, darling, you look so amazing. I knew Georgio would do a fantastic job making the dress." Sarah was standing on a white platform in the center of a white room. A tailor buzzed around her, removing pins and making sure the dress fit perfectly.

"Are you done yet?" A hairdresser, Carol, stood beside the three-sided makeup mirror, impatiently tapping a hairbrush against the palm of her hand. "I have to do her hair! We only have an hour and a half to go until ceremony time."

"Don't rush me!" the tailor chided. "The dress is the most important part of the wedding!"

"Uh, are you kidding me? Of course it's the hair! If even one strand is out of place, it'll look odd on all the pictures!" Carol shot back.

Sarah raised an eyebrow. "Umm... I think the most important are the bride and the groom."

Marina laughed heartily. "I'll have to agree with Sarah on this one."

Before the tailor or the hairdresser could retort, the bathroom door opened and Victoria, dressed in a skin-tight fit-and-flare pink dress, stepped out. "Do I look okay in this?" she questioned. "I think I look kinda chubby..." She poked at the tiny bit of stomach fat around her midsection.

"No, you look so adorable," Marina complimented Victoria as she smiled warmly. "It's a lovely dress that you picked for her, Sarah."

"Yeah, thank God you didn't pick one of the stereotypical ugly bridesmaid dresses." Victoria giggled as she spun around. "Hopefully I look good enough to attract a man," she joked. Victoria hadn't had a boyfriend in quite a while, and Sarah was always telling her to find a nice man and settle down. She had returned home from Japan for a little while, and only had a month of relaxation time in America before she had to go back.

"When I throw the bouquet, I'll aim it directly at you," Sarah promised with a grin. "Don't worry, there are plenty of attractive eligible bachelors here today. Hamilton invited a bunch of his friends."

"Ooh, handsome and successful. Just my type!" Victoria walked over to Sarah, and gave her an admiring look. "You look so amazing, Sarah. I'm a little jealous. You're about to get married in such a pretty place, you have a fiancé that adores you like crazy, you just got that job at the big magazine..." Victoria sighed happily. "I'm glad everything is working out for you."

"Vic, I'm sure you'll find the one for you soon. You know... I've noticed you checking Ryan out. You should totally go for it. He's still single, after he learned the truth about Eva and kicked her out." Sarah giggled, entertaining the thought of playing matchmaker.

"I'm thankful for that. I really hate how she lied about you threatening her, when it was really the opposite," Marina said. "I definitely approve of you with Ryan, Victoria. Lord knows he needs a sweet, wholesome girl."

Victoria blushed in response. "He wouldn't be interested in me... After all, he's got so many attractive girls chasing after him. Last I heard, he was involved with Carmen, that lingerie model!"

"You never know, Vic, you never know..." Sarah grinned. She had thought the same thing about Hamilton, and look where she was now!

"Okay, I've waited long enough!" Carol chimed in. "It's my time to shine!"

"Okay, okay," the tailor said exasperatedly, allowing Sarah to step off the platform. She sat down onto the plush seat, and stared at her reflection.

"Now you just sit there, and let me work my magic," Carol instructed firmly. She got to work, snipping, spraying and straightening. A very long forty-five minutes later, Sarah was completely dolled up. Her light hair had been tied into an elegant bun, and a sheer, flower-tipped veil was fastened to it. She had never felt so pretty and excited before in her life. She was going to be Mrs. Clouse!

"There. All finished. Don't you look marvelous?" Carol's voice returned to its usual candy sweet tone as she chirped, very pleased with her work.

"Oh, Carol, it's perfect," Marina gushed. "Hamilton is going to love it."

"Speaking of Hamilton, how is he doing? Is he nervous?" Victoria asked with a giggle.

"I want to go see him, but I know it's bad luck or something." Sarah shrugged. "But I think I'm the one that will be more nervous about this. I'm scared I'm going to mess up and say something I'm not supposed to, or trip on my dress."

Marina laughed heartily. "Oh, Sarah, don't worry, I'm sure you'll do fine."

There was a knock on the door. It opened seconds later, and the stressed face of the wedding planner peeped in. "Oh, hello, Sonya, how's it all coming along? Are we all ready for the big moment?" Victoria asked joyfully.

"Ready?! We're missing one bouquet of flowers for table 16. And one of the waiters is sick," Sonya complained as she tapped onto her phone frantically. "But don't worry, I will have it *all* sorted out. You just relax. That's what I'm here for, after all. We're starting soon though, so just be ready. Oh, also, I stopped by Hamilton in the groom's dressing room earlier, and he told me to tell you this." Sonya strode over to Sarah in her towering Christian Louboutins, and whispered something into her ear.

Sarah responded with a giggle and a blush, which made Victoria shoot her a curious stare.

"Alright. Now I have to go sort out the waiter business. I'll see you soon!" Sonya sped out as quickly as she had arrived. Ah, the life of a wedding planner was never quiet.

"What did Hamilton say?" Victoria asked.

"He said that he couldn't wait to marry me, and that he was the luckiest man in the world because he has me." Just repeating it made Sarah's lips break into a wide grin.

"Cheeeesy!" Victoria joked with a big smile blooming on her face.

"Oh, my Hamilton, he's such a sweet talker," Marina commented fondly.

The next minutes were all spent giving Sarah the final touch-ups on her makeup, making sure that she looked absolutely perfect. Sonya popped back in twenty minutes later, a big smile on her face. "I got the disaster under control. We have a new waiter, and I managed to get some new flowers for table 16. Oh, you look wonderful! Anyways, go time in ten. So get ready!"

Sarah shot everyone a nervous smile. "Alright. It's show time." She stood up, and the white dress billowed around her. The veil cascaded down her back, and she looked like a princess. "Oh, gosh, I can't believe this is actually happening. I'm so nervous."

"I'm going to go sit in the first row, with Roger. So excited! Good luck." Marina grinned as she gave

Sarah a hug, trying not to mess up her hair. "See you soon!" Marina walked out, leaving Sarah and Victoria in the room.

Victoria handed Sarah her bouquet. "Come on, let's go!" She pulled Sarah towards the door. The hallway was mostly deserted, for all the guests were already sitting in the white chairs outside. They had picked a beautiful outdoor spot for their wedding, and a nice grassy field awaited them. This quaint garden at the back of the church was definitely beautiful, and it was a gorgeous sunny day.

Sonya clattered down the church hallway. "Okay, Sarah, we're all on schedule. Hamilton and his best man Ryan are already out in the garden. Once you hear the bridal music start, just head out, okay? All eyes will be on you, but be confident. It's your big day, and no one can take that away from you! Good luck!" Sonya slipped outside after shooting Sarah a smooth wink.

Sarah swallowed dryly and fought back the instinct to lick her lips, to not ruin her lipstick. This was it. She played with a petal of one of the flowers in her bouquet of delicate white and light-purple flowers, calming herself down.

The familiar first tones of the bridal song started, and Sarah took a deep breath.

Show time!

Sonya pulled open the heavy wooden doors from outside. Everyone was standing, their heads turned towards Sarah. Big smiles were on their faces as they beamed at her. She took one nervous step towards the white stone pathway through the garden. All her friends were here, and so were his.

"You look gorgeous!" Victoria whispered from behind her. As maid of honor, she was holding the ends of Sarah's elaborate veil, making Sarah feel even more like a princess.

Sarah nodded as she began to walk with more confidence, making her way down the long path. She could see Hamilton, dressed in a completely black Armani suit, looking very handsome as he shot her a wide, lip-parting grin. Yes, this was where she was meant to be, and Hamilton was who she was meant to be with. She imagined waking up every morning next to that face, and that excited her like nothing else.

She could hear Victoria behind her, and knew that her best friend would be supporting her every step of the way. She felt lucky to have such a great friend with her on this special day. Ryan had cleaned up too, for this special day. He was wearing an equally well-cut suit, and he beamed at Sarah, then at Victoria. Hmm, maybe there really was something there after all. She would definitely keep that in mind for later, she thought to herself while suppressing a giggle.

When she reached the altar, Hamilton stepped forward and took her hands in his.

He leaned in. "You look amazing. I love you," he whispered sweetly before pulling back. His eyes flashed with affection as he smiled.

In his eyes, she could see her future, and in his hands she wanted to stay for the rest of her life. Even after all those obstacles that threatened to keep them apart, they had found their way back to each other. There were no two better suited for each other than them, and they were about to be the happiest people in the world.

"I love you too."

What to read next?

If you liked this book, you will also like *The Weekend Girlfriend.* Another interesting book is *Two Reasons to Be Single.*

The Weekend Girlfriend

Jessica has worked hard to be the paralegal that hotshot, sexy attorney Kyle needs. Unfortunately he doesn't see her as just his paralegal but also his own personal assistant. When he blames her for a mix-up in his personal life, Jessica sees no other option but to quit, thinking that her time with him is over. Much to her surprise, Kyle makes a proposition to her that she never thought she would hear coming from his lips. He needs a temporary girlfriend for his sister's wedding and he wants her to be that person. Jessica accepts the challenge and finds herself thrown into his world, learning things about him she never knew. The more time she spends with him outside of work, the more she is drawn to Kyle. As the wedding draws near, she finds herself fighting off some strong feelings for the man. When the wedding weekend is over, will Jessica be able to walk away from Kyle with her heart intact?

Two Reasons to Be Single

Olivia Parker has a job doing what she loves, a wonderful family and plenty of friends, but no luck in the love department. Tired of worrying about it, she decides to swear off love completely and focus on all the good things in her life. Just as she makes her firm resolution, Jake Harper arrives in town and knocks her plans into a tailspin. As the excited single ladies of Morning Glory surround the extremely attractive newcomer, Olivia steers clear of the "casserole brigade," as she calls the women, and tries to keep her distance from Jake. Instead, a variety of situations throw them together and they get to know each other better. They both have reasons for not wanting to get involved in a relationship, but the chemistry between them ignites, even as they desperately attempt to keep it at bay. As things heat up between Olivia and Jake, there is an aura of mystery about him that leaves Olivia certain that he is hiding something. When Jake disappears for a few days without telling Olivia that he is going out of town, she hates the way it makes her feel, and it reminds her of why she was giving up on dating in the first place. As Olivia's feelings for Jake grow, so does the need to find out what exactly brought him to Morning Glory and what he's been hiding.

About Emily Walters

Emily Walters lives in California with her beloved husband, three daughters, and two dogs. She began writing after high school, but it took her ten long years of writing for newspapers and magazines until she realized that fiction is her real passion. Emily likes to create a mental movie in her reader's mind about charismatic characters, their passionate relationships and interesting adventures. When she isn't writing romantic stories, she can be found reading a fiction book, jogging, or traveling with her family. She loves Starbucks, Matt Damon and Argentinian tango.

One Last Thing...

If you believe that *Christmas Embrace* is worth sharing, would you spend a minute to let your friends know about it?

If this book lets them have a great time, they will be enormously grateful to you – as will I.

Emily

www.EmilyWaltersBooks.com

Printed in Great Britain
by Amazon